英漢對照

布雷克詩選
Selected Poems of William Blake
William Blake 著　張熾恆 譯

第二版

布雷克詩選
Selected Poems of William Blake
William Blake 著　張熾恆 譯

國家圖書館出版品預行編目資料

布雷克詩選 = Selected Poems of William Blake
／William Blake 著，張熾恆譯；二版.--臺北市：
書林, 2024 面; 公分 --
ISBN 978-626-7193-90-7（平裝）

873.51   113014118

布雷克詩選（第二版）
Selected Poems of William Blake 2nd Edition

作　　　者	William Blake
譯　　　者	張熾恆
執 行 編 輯	陳衍秀
出　版　者	書林出版有限公司
	100 臺北市羅斯福路四段 60 號 3 樓
	Tel (02) 2368-4938．2365-8617 Fax (02) 2368-8929．2363-6630
臺北書林書店	106 臺北市新生南路三段 88 號 2 樓之 5 Tel (02) 2365-8617
學校業務部	Tel (02) 2368-7226．(04) 2376-3799．(07) 229-0300
經銷業務部	Tel (02) 2368-4938
發　行　人	蘇正隆
郵　　　撥	15743873．書林出版有限公司
網　　　址	http://www.bookman.com.tw
經 銷 代 理	紅螞蟻圖書有限公司
	臺北市內湖區舊宗路二段 121 巷 19 號
	Tel (02) 2795-3656（代表號）Fax (02) 2795-4100
登 記 證	局版台業字第一八三一號
出 版 日 期	2007 年 4 月一版，2024 年 10 月二版初刷
定　　　價	350 元
I S B N	978-626-7193-90-7

Chinese translation, notes, and introduction by Chiheng Zhang
Copyright © 2007 by Bookman Books, Ltd. All rights reserved.
No part of this publication may be reproduced or transmitted in any form or by any means, without permission.

欲利用本書全部或部分內容者，須徵得書林出版有限公司同意或書面授權。

William Blake,《喜悅之日》(*Glad Day*),又名《阿爾比恩之舞》(*The Dance of Albion*),1793 英國古稱阿爾比恩 (Albion)。布雷克的神人 (the human form divine) 意象是力與美、光與昇華、政治與精神自由的象徵。

Selected Poems of William Blake

Contents

Preface ···1
Poetical Sketches (1783)
    To Spring ···18
    To Summer···20
    To Autumn ···22
    To Winter ···24
    To the Evening Star ··26
    To Morning ··26
    Fair Elenor ···28
    Song: "How Sweet I roam'd from field to field" ···············36
    Song: "My silks and fine array" ··38
    Song: "Love and harmony combine" ··································40
    Song: "I love the jocund dance" ··42
    Song: "Memory, hither come" ··44
    Mad Song···46
    Song: "Fresh from the dewy hill, the merry year" ············48
    Song: "When early morn walks forth in sober grey" ·········50
    To the Muses···52
    Gwin, King of Norway ···54
    Song by a Shepherd (c.1787)···66
    Song by an Old Shepherd ··66
Songs of Innocence and of Experience (1794)
Songs of Innocence (1789)
    Introduction ··72

II

目錄

譯者序：預言人類精神世界的先知 ……………………1

詩的素描（1783）
　　春之詠 ……………………………………19
　　夏之詠 ……………………………………21
　　秋之詠 ……………………………………23
　　冬之詠 ……………………………………25
　　晚星之詠 …………………………………27
　　黎明之詠 …………………………………27
　　美麗的愛莉諾 ……………………………29
　　歌：多麼快活 ……………………………37
　　歌：我的綢衣 ……………………………39
　　歌：愛情與和諧 …………………………41
　　歌：我愛 …………………………………43
　　歌：記憶，到這裡來 ……………………45
　　瘋狂之歌 …………………………………47
　　歌：從綴滿露珠的山崗 …………………49
　　歌：當晨曦 ………………………………51
　　致繆斯 ……………………………………53
　　圭恩，挪威王 ……………………………55
　　牧人之歌 …………………………………67
　　老牧人之歌 ………………………………67

天真與經驗之歌（1794）
天真之歌（1789）
　　序詩 ………………………………………73

Selected Poems of William Blake

    The Shepherd ··74
    The Echoing Green ···74
    The Lamb ··78
    The Little Black Boy ··80
    The Blossom ··82
    The Chimney Sweeper ··84
    The Little Boy Lost ···86
    The Little Boy Found ···88
    Laughing Song ··88
    A Cradle Song ··90
    The Divine Image ···94
    Holy Thursday ··96
    Night ···96
    Spring ··102
    Nurse's Song ··104
    Infant Joy ··106
    A Dream ···106
    On Another's Sorrow ···110

Songs of Experience (1794)
    Introduction ··118
    Earth's Answer ···120
    The Clod and the Pebble ··122
    Holy Thursday ··124
    The Little Girl Lost ···126
    The Little Girl Found ··130
    The Chimney Sweeper ··136
    Nurse's Song ··138

牧羊人························75
回音草坪······················75
羔羊··························79
黑人小孩······················81
鮮花··························83
掃煙囪的孩子··················85
男童之失······················87
男童之得······················89
笑歌··························89
搖籃曲························91
至上的形象····················95
升天節························97
夜····························97
春···························103
保母之歌·····················105
童稚的歡樂···················107
一個夢·······················107
對別人的悲傷·················111

經驗之歌（1794）

序詩·························119
大地的回答···················121
土塊和卵石···················123
升天節·······················125
幼女之失·····················127
幼女之得·····················131
掃煙囪的孩子·················137
保母之歌·····················139

v

Selected Poems of William Blake

    The Sick Rose ·················138
    The Fly ·················140
    The Angel ·················142
    The Tiger ·················144
    My Pretty Rose Tree ·················146
    Ah! Sun-Flower ·················146
    The Lilly ·················148
    The Garden of Love ·················148
    The Little Vagabond ·················150
    London ·················152
    The Human Abstract ·················154
    Infant Sorrow ·················156
    A Poison Tree ·················158
    A Little Boy Lost ·················160
    A Little Girl Lost ·················162
    To Tirzah ·················166
    The Schoolboy ·················168
    The Voice of the Ancient Bard ·················170
    A Divine Image ·················172

The Book of Thel (1789-1791)
    Thel's Motto ·················176

Visions of the Daughters of Albion (1793)
    The Argument ·················192
    Visions ·················192

The Marriage of Heaven and Hell (1790-1793)
    The Argument ·················216
    The Voice of the Devil ·················220

枯萎的玫瑰	139
蠅	141
天使	143
虎	145
我美麗的玫瑰樹	147
太陽花	147
百合	149
愛的花園	149
小流浪者	151
倫敦	153
人之抽象	155
嬰兒的悲傷	157
有毒的樹	159
少年之失	161
少女之失	163
致特拉	167
小學生	169
古代吟遊詩人之聲	171
至上的形象	173

塞爾書（1789-1791）
| 塞爾的警句 | 177 |

阿爾比恩女兒們的夢幻（1793）
| 梗概 | 193 |
| 夢幻 | 193 |

天國與地獄的婚姻（1790-1793）
| 引子 | 217 |
| 魔王的聲音 | 221 |

Selected Poems of William Blake

A Memorable Fancy ··224
Proverbs of Hell ···224
A Memorable Fancy ··234
A Memorable Fancy ··240
A Memorable Fancy ··242
A Memorable Fancy ··252
A Song of Liberty (1792) ···259
Notebook : manuscripts (1793-1818)
The Smile ··268
The Land of Dreams ···270
The Crystal Cabinet ··272
Auguries of Innocence ··274
William Bond ···288
Morning ··294
The Birds ··294
"Why was Cupid a Boy" ···296
"I rose up at the dawn of day" ···300
"Never seek to tell thy love" ··302
"I laid me down upon a bank" ···304
"I saw a chapel all of gold" ···304
"I heard an Angel singing" ··306
A Cradle Song ···308
"I fear'd the fury of my wind" ··310
"Why should I care for the men of Thames" ····························312
Silent, Silent Night ··312
"O lapwing thou fliest around the heath" ·································314
"Thou hast a lap full of seed" ··314

一個難忘的幻象 ················ 225
　　地獄的箴言 ·················· 225
　　一個難忘的幻象 ················ 235
　　一個難忘的幻象 ················ 241
　　一個難忘的幻象 ················ 243
　　一個難忘的幻象 ················ 253
自由之歌（1792） ················· **259**
筆記本・手稿詩選（1793-1818）
　　微笑 ····················· 269
　　夢國 ····················· 271
　　水晶櫃 ···················· 273
　　天眞之預言術 ················· 275
　　威廉・勃德 ·················· 289
　　晨 ······················ 295
　　鳥 ······················ 295
　　爲什麼丘比特是個男孩 ············· 297
　　我在晨光熹微中起身 ·············· 301
　　別試圖吐露你的愛情 ·············· 303
　　我躺倒在一處河岸上面 ············· 305
　　我看見一座全金的教堂 ············· 305
　　在黎明升起的時候 ··············· 307
　　搖籃曲 ···················· 309
　　我怕我的風兒的猛烈 ·············· 311
　　我爲什麼要介意 ················ 313
　　靜謐的，靜謐的夜 ··············· 313
　　啊，田鳧 ··················· 315
　　你有個裝滿種子的裙兜 ············· 315

The Wild Flower's Song 316
To Nobodaddy 318
[How to know Love from Deceit] 318
"Deceit to secrecy confined" 320
"There souls of men are bougth and sold" 320
Day 322
"If you trap the moment before its ripe" 322
Eternity 322
"The look of love alarms" 324
"My Spectre around me night & day" 324
"I saw a monk of Charlemaine" 332
"Mock on, Mock on, Voltaire, Rousseau" 338
"You don't believe" 338
"Now Art has lost its mental Charms" 340
The Golden Net 342
The Mental Traveller 344
"Great things are done when Men & Mountains meet" 354
To God 354
"Terror in the house does roar" 354
And did those feet in ancient time 356
Chronology 358
Related Sites 361

野花之歌 ·················· 317
致諾巴達底 ·················· 319
「愛情對缺點永遠盲目」 ·················· 319
虛偽受隱秘之制約 ·················· 321
那裡在買賣人的靈魂 ·················· 321
白晝 ·················· 323
假如 ·················· 323
永恆 ·················· 323
愛情的神態使人驚恐 ·················· 325
我的幽靈 ·················· 325
查理曼的修士 ·················· 333
嘲笑吧,嘲笑吧,伏爾泰、盧梭 ·················· 339
你不信 ·················· 339
藝術已失去了內在的魅力 ·················· 341
金網 ·················· 343
內心旅行者 ·················· 345
偉大的事業 ·················· 355
致上帝 ·················· 355
恐怖與慈悲 ·················· 355
要是遠古時那些聖足 ·················· 357

布雷克年表 ·················· 358
好站拾穗 ·················· 361

譯者序：預言人類精神世界的先知

我願意以人子和詩人的名義，而不是以學者或譯者的名義向你奉獻這本詩集，作者是一個我們知道得太少的詩人。在了解他和他的詩之後，我們將意識到，忽視他，對於詩歌，尤其是外國詩的讀者是一個多麼大的缺憾；對於外國文學的介紹和研究工作是一個多麼大的缺陷。

他是一位十八世紀末葉和十九世紀初葉的英國詩人，全名威廉·布雷克。從文學史上來說，屬於前浪漫主義時代，雖然他與這個「主義」並不相干。即便在其祖國、在歐美，也有很長的時間沒有得到足夠的重視；他在世時，只有華茲華斯（William Wordsworth, 1770-1850）等少數人注意到他，並且受了他的影響。直到十九世紀中葉以後，他才聲譽日增，原因在於他遠遠地超越了他的時代。這位生前備受冷落的詩人，從此成了評論界的寵兒、大師所效法的大師。正如威特卡特 (W.P. Witcutt) 在《布雷克之心理學研究》(*Blake, a Psychological Study*)一書中所說：「雪萊、濟慈、華茲華斯和柯立芝的聲名依然如舊，拜倫的聲譽已不如他在世之時，騷塞已經被人們遺忘；而布雷克的聲望卻與日俱增。」

英國二十世紀最偉大的詩人葉慈 (W.B. Yeats, 1865-1939) 從1887年起開始編輯布雷克的詩作，並且受到他很大的影響，他模仿布雷克，創造了一個自己的宗教神話體系。

美國二十世紀的大詩人之一，艾略特（T.S. Eliot, 1888-1965) 曾專注地研究布雷克，「向布雷克學到了不少東西」。

Selected Poems of William Blake

　　一些批評家在論述詩歌發展史時指出，布雷克和華茲華斯是英語詩歌革命的先鋒；另一些評論家在褒揚艾略特時，將艾略特和布雷克、華茲華斯並稱爲英語詩歌革命的三大開路先鋒。

　　布雷克，布雷克，布雷克是一個什麼樣的詩人？我們難以很快地回答，因爲我們也許已經意識到，他是英國文學史上最獨特、最複雜的詩人。

一、純真的人，神聖的瘋子

　　布雷克首先是個人，然後才是詩人。

　　許多人爲他畫過像。初次見到他的像，你一定會被震懾住：這是一張多麼不尋常的臉啊！他異常寬闊明朗的前額，他那雙目光如炬、略顯驚惶的大眼睛。當你再次看他，你會看到他眼裡的智慧、專注、瘋狂和純真。他跨越世紀，注視著自己預言過的世界。

　　1757年，他出生於倫敦一個貧寒的襪商家庭，從小就「富於幻想，神經過敏」。四歲時他見到上帝；另一次，他又看到田野裡一棵大樹上棲滿了天使。類似的經歷是在他三十歲的時候，十九歲的弟弟羅伯特‧布雷克患病夭折，他見到弟弟的靈魂冉冉上升，穿過屋頂，升向天空，於是樂而忘悲，擊掌相應，欣然歌誦。最後一次，是他臨終的時候，他無比安詳，面帶歡樂的笑容，吟唱著他在天國所見的景物。這種「神跡」般的經歷，無論意味著什麼，至少告訴我們一件事：他是個虔誠的人。我們還會發現，他確實超脫了世俗。

　　他沒有接受正規教育。原因不是家境貧寒，而是他的個

譯者序：預言人類精神世界的先知

性。他不喜歡正統學校的壓抑氣氛，拒絕入學。這時他還非常年幼，而他極強的個性已經開始顯露。他「對任何使他受約束的企圖，都以不可遏止的憤怒來反抗」。幸好，他的父母雖然是普通市民和小商人，卻非常開明，聽憑他不進學校，在家中學習他喜歡的東西。對於布雷克，這是難得的幸運，卻也給他日後的生活留下隱患。這意味著他將沒有閱世能力，與世俗格格不入。

他所喜歡的是繪畫和詩歌。他十一歲進繪畫學校，十二歲開始寫詩，那些詩後來收入了《詩的素描》。他在繪畫學校三年多，表現出非凡的藝術才能，父親預備讓他師從一位著名的畫家。但是，為了不影響父親的小本生意和弟妹的前途，他主動放棄了這個求之不得的機會，跟隨一位雕刻家當學徒。那一年，他才十四歲！這個單純的人！

他終身靠繪畫和雕刻維生，詩歌從未給他的清貧生活任何補貼。他的第一部詩集是靠朋友的資助印成鉛字的。他的一生便是繪畫和雕刻創作，收取稿酬或出售；以及創作詩歌，配上自己的插圖出版，由自己或別人譜上曲子，在朋友的沙龍裡詠唱。只有一個例外：二十七歲時父親去世，他和弟弟一同開了一家印刷店，一年後印刷店破產，從此他再也沒有謀過別的生計。因為生活所迫，他不斷地搬家，最遠曾經搬到蘇格蘭。有時，他靠別人的資助生活，但從不妥協，從不出賣自己。

他一生最大的幸運是他的婚姻。二十一歲時，他因追求一位輕浮的姑娘而失戀。這時，有位鄰家姑娘真摯地向他表示了同情。她的名字叫凱瑟琳·布歇爾 (Catherine Boucher)，本人是文盲，父親是菜農。四年以後，布雷克經

3

Selected Poems of William Blake

濟獨立，克服家庭的阻力，使她的姓名變成凱瑟琳·布雷克。布雷克夫婦沒有子嗣。溫柔的妻子成了他一生的忠實伴侶和唯一的安慰。他教會她讀書、寫字和製版技術，使她成了他最忠實的助手；同時，他也忠於妻子。這是他與其他詩人不同的地方，他的一生中從未有過緋聞，從未拜倒在別的貴婦人腳下！

　　他果敢無畏。在那個時代，英國是反對法國大革命的大本營。然而，他卻敢寫詩歌頌法國革命。著名出版商約瑟夫·約翰遜(Joseph Johnson) 敢印行瑪麗·沃爾斯考夫特 (Mary Wollstonecraft, 1759-1797)的《為女權辯護》(*A Vindication of the Rights of Women*) 和葛德文 (William Godwin, 1756-1836) 的《政治正義論》(*Political Justice*)，可是當他印完布雷克的《法國革命》(*The French Revolution*)第一卷後，竟不敢拿到市場上去賣！

　　在《天國與地獄的婚姻》(*The Marriage of Heaven and Hell*)中，他竟然否定代表理性的上帝，讚美代表力的撒旦，並且宣稱、預言了上帝的退位：「永恆的地獄復興了……現在是艾登在統治，是回到伊甸園的亞當。」他希望天國與地獄結合，成為理想的人世！

　　客居薩塞克斯郡 (Sussex) 的菲芬 (Felpham) 時，他曾憤怒地將一名警員逐出花園，被控犯了挑起暴動、威脅國王罪。幾個月後，他在法庭上慷慨陳詞，在聽審者的歡呼聲中被判無罪釋放。

　　他的一生就是工作。倫威克 (W. L. Renwick) 在《1789至1815年間的英國文學》 (*English Literature, 1789-1815*) 中說：「威廉·布雷克的一生質樸無奇，以雕刻家知名於世。

譯者序：預言人類精神世界的先知

他和出版商關係融洽；經常出入於藝術家之間，他們把他視為其中一員；他有一些愛他、並且幫助他的朋友。他的編年史極其簡單，傳記上幾乎沒有什麼可以大書特書，只有持續的藝術創作。他的生活是一個統一的整體，從中我們只能看出雕刻作品、情感關係和哲學思想上的變化。」簡單地說，布雷克是一個單純的人，過著單純的生活，他一生中最主要的活動就是藝術創作。直到去世前幾天，他仍然在工作。「他叫人用最後幾個先令去買碳筆」，畫完最後一幅畫後說道：「我已經盡力而為了。」這就是他的遺言。

　　1855年，撒繆爾·帕爾墨 (Samuel Palmer, 1805-1881) 在致友人書信中說：「布雷克，你見過他一次，便永遠不會忘記。他的知識博大精深，談吐非凡，但有些神經質……和他一起在鄉間散步，就是在接受美的靈魂……他是一個不戴面具的人……他是那種我們在整個生命旅程中所遇見的一位絕無僅有的人。」這就是布雷克：沒有受過正規教育，一生清貧，但擁有最獨立可敬的人格、傑出天賦和非凡才能；生前沒有顯赫的聲名，但毫不介意沉溺於自己的藝術世界和精神世界。

　　他脫俗，但是不放浪形骸。他只是有些「瘋狂」。他綽號就是「神聖的瘋子」。他讓人想起美國著名的黑色幽默小說家馮尼古特 (Kurt Vonnegut, 1922-) 的《上帝保佑你，羅斯瓦特先生》(*God Bless You, Mr. Rosewater*) 中的「瘋子」，神聖的瘋子。那部小說多次引用布雷克的詩句，而且只引用了布雷克的詩。他不放浪形骸，他很專注認真。他認真地瘋，他在追求什麼？

　　「布雷克當然捲入了男人、女人和他們的社會所組成的

Selected Poems of William Blake

普通世界,但他一直固守他稱之為『想像』的永恆世界的非凡價值與非凡真實,可以說他一生都企圖把這兩個世界合而為一,並且展示給別人。」

二、不僅是詩人

布雷克生活在一個「憤怒與喧囂」的時代。英國工業領先全世界而迅速發展,一方面使許多人失業,陷入貧困,另一方面對文藝發展造成了巨大的衝擊;而法國革命和美國獨立戰爭相繼爆發,也喚醒了詩人們的叛逆意識,為十九世紀浪漫主義的興起提供了條件。但是菲爾丁 (Henry Fielding, 1707-1754) 和哥爾斯密 (Oliver Goldsmith, 1730-1774) 的時代已經過去,文學處於這兩個波峰之間,詩人們普遍感到壓抑和困惑。布雷克的時代把絕大多數詩歌逼進了憂鬱的孤寂之地和瘋人院。

作為一個詩人,布雷克在這種環境的壓迫之下不斷成熟。一開始,他對革命感到歡欣鼓舞,顯得樂觀堅定;但不久之後,現實使他處處碰壁,在外在世界裡,他被打敗了。然而,他卻沒有在精神上被打敗,並沒有使自己的詩歌變成宣洩不滿情緒的下水道。他從外在現實進入了心靈現實,而不是進入了「憂鬱的孤寂之地和瘋人院」,這是他有別於同時代詩人的偉大之處。革命對他來說僅僅是「一種思想,一種內在世界、精神世界」,他在這個世界裡進行戰鬥:

把我那灼亮的金弓帶給我,
把我那願望的箭矢帶給我,
帶給我長矛!招展的雲彩呀!

譯者序：預言人類精神世界的先知

把我那烈火的戰車帶給我！

我不會停止內心的戰鬥，
我的劍也不會在手中安眠，
直到我們建立起耶路撒冷，
在英格蘭青翠而快樂的地面。

這種追求不但造就了他超越時代的詩歌，而且使他本人成了一個預言家。他從一個見過上帝和天使、見過靈魂升天的夢幻者，變成用無韻詩體、象徵性語言來預言上帝退位，預言人類精神世界之變化的先知。他所預言的不是外在世界的變化，而是人類精神世界的未來。他用一種奇特的語言，在二百年前，預言了今日世界人們在宗教和哲學觀念上的變化，包括性的解放。這一點，在本詩集所選的《阿爾比恩女兒們的夢幻》(*Visions of the Daughters of Albion*) 中可以看到。

因此，他不但是詩人，還是預言家。1927年「人人叢書」(Everyman's Library) 版的布雷克作品集，書名就叫《布雷克詩與預言集》(*William Blake's Poems and Prophecies*)。同時，他也是一位著名的雕刻家，在世時主要以繪畫和雕刻聞名，十八歲時即為著名的西敏寺作畫，最擅長的是銅版蝕刻，那是他表達思想、幻想和精神世界的另一種語言。他為自己的詩卷配上了精美的插圖，並且曾應出版商之邀，為許多著名小說家和詩人的作品集製作插圖。

他為詩人托馬斯·格雷 (Thomas Gray, 1716-1771) 的《詩集》(*Poems*)、彌爾頓(John Milton, 1608-1674)的《失樂園》

(*Paradise Lost*) 和《復樂園》(*Paradise Regained*)、喬叟 (Geoffrey Chaucer, 1343-1400) 的《坎特伯里故事集》(*The Canterbury Tales*)、班揚 (John Bunyan, 1628-1688) 的《天路歷程》(*The Pilgrim's Progress*)、華茲華斯的《詩集》(*Poems*)、但丁 (Dante, 1265-1321) 的《神曲》(*The Divine Comedy*)……作了大量想像力極其豐富的精美插圖。

這些作品多為宗教題材。畫面上有人，有神；有正統宗教的神，更有他自己宗教系統中的神。它們飽滿、強壯、有時又扭曲的形象，自有一種與眾不同的力量；它們所洋溢、迸發的，是他超凡卻有些怪異和瘋狂的想像之美。扭曲、綻開、翅膀、飛翔、光、輝煌、昇華……到底是什麼？他表現的，正是他所讚美的力與美。

對於他的雕刻繪畫創作，在他去世後一年，約翰・托馬斯・史密斯(John Thomas Smith, 1766-1833) 說：「我堅定地相信，沒有一個藝術家能像他那樣，一點都不剽竊別人的作品。」

他的詩，他的預言，再加上他的雕刻，勾勒出他的藝術世界和精神世界的輪廓。

三、宗教、哲學和詩歌

他的作品所展現的，不僅是他的藝術世界，也是他的精神世界。從表象上來看，他的作品是詩歌、預言和雕刻三位一體；從本質上來看，他的作品是宗教、哲學和詩歌三位一體。

有人說過，哲學和詩歌永遠走不到一起。但是，在布雷克的詩中，我們看到了哲學和詩歌比較完美的結合。我們可

譯者序：預言人類精神世界的先知

以將《天眞之歌》與《經驗之歌》(Songs of Innocence and of Experience) 比較一下。這兩部分許多詩題是相同的，或至少相互呼應。它們都是非常質樸、非常具體（少數例外）的詩，然而對應的兩首詩放在一起，卻體現了兩種對立的狀態或哲學。這種特殊的形式爲詩與哲學的結合提供了契機，使哲學進入了詩，詩避免了說教。

布雷克從不說教，從不誇示自己的智慧，他並不認爲自己有大智慧。他將一切付諸想像與形象。他著魔似地沉溺於自己的想像，幾乎脫離了外在世界，他直接追求內在性。對於詩人，這是一種大智慧。這是一種哲學意義上的革命。可嘆的是它發生在浪漫主義與現實主義之前。相對於浪漫主義，它沒有心理與情緒的誇張，沒有過度的宣洩；相對於現實主義而言，它更爲直接地訴諸事物的本質和心靈的眞實，努力掙脫現象的束縛，這正是現代主義的基本特徵之一。

然而，布雷克沒有自己的哲學系統（在哲學上他受斯威頓伯格 [Emanuel Swedenborg, 1688-1772] 的影響較深），而是發展了自己的宗教系統。這是又一種革命：他創造了自己的宗教系統，這個系統被冠以《先知書》(Illuminated Books) 之名。代表作除了前面提過的作品之外，還包括譯本中選入的《塞爾書》(The Book of Thel) 和其他許多作品，其中最主要的是他的長篇巨著《四天神》(The Four Zoas)。這四位「天神」是：尤利壬(Urizen)——理性，魯法(Luvah)——感情，塔馬斯 (Tharmas)——力量，尤索納 (Urthona)——心靈。布雷克認爲，在「經驗」世界裡，人已經分裂爲這四個部分，《四天神》的主要內容便是這四個部分之間的鬥爭，他期望這四個部分在永恆的理想世界中重新合而爲一。這便是他的宗教

Selected Poems of William Blake

核心，仍然是「天真」與「經驗」的問題。在布雷克那裡，沒有詩歌、哲學與宗教之間的關係問題。一切合為一體，從他的心靈出發，統一於他的詩與畫。

我們是否想到了前些年很時髦的「異化」(alienation) 一詞？其實兩百年之前，它在布雷克筆下就已經出現了。不過，那不是時髦，而是一種痛苦，痛苦變成了宗教。

四、虎！虎！

只能說我們對布雷克了解得不夠，不能說我們不知道布雷克。大概所有了解外國文學的人都知道他的〈倫敦〉(London)和〈虎〉(The Tiger)。〈虎〉是布雷克的不朽之作，但它前兩行的所有中文翻譯都是錯的，而且錯得離譜。

我有意在此指出這個錯誤，同時想說，對布雷克作品極有限的譯作中錯了不少。文學翻譯現在錯得太多、太令人憂慮。我企圖通過糾正這個錯誤來進入一個重要的話題。原文似乎是兩行太簡單的文字：

Tiger! Tiger! burning bright,
In the Forests of the Night.

譯文一：
老虎！老虎！你金色輝煌，
火似地照亮黑夜的林莽，

譯文二：
老虎！老虎！你熾烈地發光，

譯者序：預言人類精神世界的先知

照得夜晚的森林燦爛輝煌。

譯文一只不過沒有完全掌握原文，譯文二簡直是把原文當打油詩了。且不談「多」：「金色」當然是加上去的，多了意思的「林莽」是為了押韻，布雷克也沒有說「照亮」森林。只說「少」：少了 burning（燃燒），少了 Forests 的大寫 F 和 Night 的大寫 N。如果只是輝煌和放光，為什麼布雷克不說 shining bright 呢？如果只是黑夜的林莽或黑夜的森林，為什麼布雷克說 the Forests of the Night 而不說 the forests in the night 呢？布雷克為什麼要大寫？少的恰恰是最關鍵的東西。

因為布雷克是在象徵，而不是在比喻。所以，是「黑夜之林」，如同但丁的《神曲》；而不是「黑夜的林莽」或「夜晚的森林」。他用的是後來「意象派」詩人所說的「直接」原則：不是「像」，而是「直接就是」。不是「火似地照亮」，而是「燃燒」：burn 這個詞並沒有別的解釋。這兩行詩不妨譯成：

虎！虎！光焰灼灼，
燃燒在黑夜之林。

順便提一下，這兩行詩的音步，雖可讀作44，但按照英詩格律，第二行詩更應看作43或42，因為沒有重音不成音步；並且，嚴格來說，布雷克在這裡並沒有嚴格遵循格律。布雷克原本就是傳統的反叛者和革命者，他的詩，有時嚴格押韻，音步勉強，不成格（抑揚或抑抑揚等）；他還開創了大量用無韻體寫詩的先河。反過來，如果他過於拘泥於表面

Selected Poems of William Blake

形式,他的詩如何能如此精準地表達他靈魂的奔放不羈!同樣,如果譯詩過於拘泥於原詩的表面形式,如何能準確表達原詩的靈魂!既然如此,原詩的aabb韻腳譯成abcc又有何不可,較之於盡失原詩之精髓,何足道哉!

我們從兩行原文中窺見了布雷克詩的特色。現代著名文學批評家沃倫 (Robert Penn Warren, 1905-1989) 在討論意象、隱喻、象徵和神話時說:「布雷克的『老虎』就是一種神秘的隱喻」,這種隱喻「和人把自己投射到非人世界的隱喻恰恰背道而馳」。因此,布雷克的老虎是「作者心目中一個幻想的生物,既是事物,也是象徵」。

他的確說得非常中肯。布雷克的「虎」是虎而非虎,但不能說是一種比喻。否則,比喻什麼?它是一種象徵。不像什麼,它「直接就是」。因此有人說布雷克是神秘主義者,但他的「神秘主義」不是正統宗教的神秘主義。他的隱喻既不像《聖經》中的隱喻,也不是玄學派詩人那種讓人摸不著頭腦的隱喻。的確,他是在象徵。布雷克的詩,尤其是後期的詩中,很少出現like這個字。象徵構成了屬於他自己的詩體與宗教神話系統。

布雷克的詩質樸(早期的《詩的素描》除外)、清新,但最主要的特點,也是使他稱得上大師的特點之一,是他的詩歌具有美妙的音樂性。前面提到過,他把自己的詩譜上曲子吟唱。其實,它們本身就是音樂。泰戈爾 (Rabindranath Tagore, 1861-1941) 在《一個藝術家的宗教》(*The Religion of an Artist*) 中曾舉他手稿中的一首詩為例:

別試圖吐露你的愛情——

譯者序：預言人類精神世界的先知

那不能吐露的愛情；
因為那和風輕輕飄移，
默默地，不露形跡。

我吐露了愛，我吐露了愛，
我把整個心表白；
打著冷顫，萬分地恐懼——
唉！她啟步離去。

她剛剛從我身邊離去，
就有個旅人走過；
他不言不語，不露形跡，
嘆一聲就將她俘獲。

　　整首詩宛若一陣清風，「不露形跡」地輕輕飄過。再如他的〈笑歌〉(Laughing Song) 就像一條「哈——哈——」地歡笑著奔騰而過的溪流；他的〈致繆斯〉(To the Muses) 就像一根游絲，緩緩游移著，直到最後才突然迸發出壓抑的情感。他的〈虎〉的節奏則是如此鏗鏘有力，如此明快，一瀉到底，韻味無窮：

虎，虎，光焰灼灼，
燃燒在黑夜之林；
怎樣的神手和神眼
構造你可畏的美健？

Selected Poems of William Blake

五、現代主義的預言者

我曾經用這個題目寫過一篇文章（見《外國文學評論》1989年第四期）。在這裡，已經沒有必要再多說什麼，我只是覺得，這個題目很適合用來結束這篇不太合乎常規的序言——我不想把它寫成一篇面面俱到的、論證式的論文。其實，說到這裡，我們已經對詩人的獨特性和複雜性有了一個大致的認識。

也許，需要多說幾句的是，本質上，詩歌是生命的一部分。詩歌使所有的人，無論在時間和空間上相隔多遠，只要願意，都能在心靈上溝通。而布雷克，因為他的執著與「瘋狂」，因為他奇特的想像和預見，在許多詩人中，更能跨越時間和空間，與現代的詩人、現代的讀者相會——如果你願意稍稍深入他的詩歌和他的精神。

現代人所體驗的正是在「經驗」世界中感受到的壓抑、惶惑和失落。我們所體驗的現代文明的痛苦和失落，他體驗得太早。他所尋求的答案，我們仍然在尋求。他永恆的理想世界，太執著於追求精神世界。也許，今天物質世界壓倒精神世界的力量過於強大，所以我們沒有他那麼執著和敏感，那是一件太痛苦的事。但在他的精神世界裡，並沒有否定物質和肉體。相反的，他所預言和讚美的，也許正是現代文明的特徵。

蕭伯納 (George Bernard Shaw, 1856-1950) 對我們說：「歐文 (Robert Owen, 1771-1858)、巴特勒(Samuel Butler, 1835-1902)、王爾德 (Oscar Wilde, 1854-1900)、尼采 (Friedrich Nietzsche, 1844-1900) 和其他人都是不自覺的布雷克主義者。他是正在到來的時代的靈魂，道德革命的先驅，

譯者序：預言人類精神世界的先知

他寫下了革命的聖經。」在這個「革命的聖經」——《天國與地獄的婚姻》中，他讓亞當來統治世界，讓魔王撒旦出來反對上帝。他讓魔王和地獄宣稱：

「生存的一部分就是創造力的富有。」
「力是唯一的生命，來自肉體；理性是力之界限或外圍。」
「力是永恆的歡樂。」
「生機勃勃就是美。」
「現在得到證實的事情曾經只是幻想。」
「山羊的淫慾是上帝的慷慨。」
「女人的裸體是上帝的傑作。」

他還說：「夠了！或許太多了！」

布雷克，詩人，「神聖的瘋子」，象徵者，神秘主義者，叛逆者，預言者。對待這樣一個詩人，是不敢也絕不能輕率的。這本選集的翻譯自1981年始，1983年完成初稿，其後十五年中，又歷經多次修改。把它奉獻出來，為的是翻譯和介紹外國詩歌，也為了不應被忽視的詩人，為了詩歌的讀者和詩歌本身。

我想，為了這些目的，斷斷續續花費多年勞動，是值得的。

張熾恆
1998年5月於上海棚居

Selected Poems of William Blake

1783

Poetical Sketches

詩的素描

William Blake, *For Children: The Gates of Paradise*, object 1, 1793

To Spring

O thou, with dewy locks, who lookest down
Thro' the clear windows of the morning, turn
Thine angel eyes upon our western isle,
Which in full choir hails thy approach, O Spring!

The hills tell each other, and the list'ning
Vallies hear; all our longing eyes are turned
Up to thy bright pavillions: issue forth,
And let thy holy feet visit our clime.

Come o'er the eastern hills, and let our winds
Kiss thy perfumed garments; let us taste
Thy morn and evening breath; scatter thy pearls
Upon our love-sick land that mourns for thee.

O deck her forth with thy fair fingers; pour
Thy soft kisses on her bosom; and put
Thy golden crown upon her languish'd head,
Whose modest tresses were bound up for thee!

春之詠

你啊,髮卷綴晨露;俯望的臉
透出明淨晨窗,你天使的目光
快請投向我們這西方的島嶼,它整個地
揚起合唱的歌聲歡呼你,啊春天!

山巒互相轉告,溪谷凝神
傾聽;所有我們渴求的目光
都投向你輝煌的篷帳:出來吧,
邁著你神聖的步履前來造訪——

越東方的山巒而來,讓我們的風
吻你芬芳的衣裳;讓我們品嘗
你清晨和黃昏的呼吸,灑你的珍珠
在這塊為你苦苦相思的土地上。

哦,請用你的柔指將她裝扮,
把你的柔吻傾注在她的胸懷;
把金色花冠戴在她焦思的頭上,
她素樸的秀髮已為你束了起來!

To Summer

O thou, who passest thro' our vallies in
Thy strength, curb thy fierce steeds, allay the heat
That flames from their large nostrils! thou, O Summer,
Oft pitched'st here thy golden tent, and oft
Beneath our oaks hast slept, while we beheld
With joy, thy ruddy limbs and flourishing hair.

Beneath our thickest shades we oft have heard
Thy voice, when noon upon his fervid car
Rode o'er the deep of heaven; beside our springs
Sit down, and in our mossy vallies, on
Some bank beside a river clear, throw thy
Silk draperies off, and rush into the stream:
Our vallies love the Summer in his pride.

Our bards are fam'd who strike the silver wire:
Our youths are bolder than the southern swains:
Our maidens fairer in the sprightly dance:
We lack not songs, nor instruments of joy,
Nor echoes sweet, nor waters clear as heaven,
Nor laurel wreaths against the sultry heat.

夏之詠

你啊,以強力穿過我們的溪谷,
請勒住你的烈馬,讓它們的巨鼻
少噴出些灼熱的鼻息!你啊,夏,
常在此搭起金色的帳篷,常常
入眠在橡樹下,那時我們快樂地
注視著你紅潤的肢體和茂密的頭髮。

當正午乘火輦在高遠的藍天上奔馳,
在濃密的綠陰下,我們時常能夠
聽到你的聲音。在我們的泉邊
坐下吧;在這青苔如茵的溪谷裡,
在這清澈的小河邊,把你的綢衣
拋在一旁,扎進那潺潺清流:
我們的溪谷熱愛盛極的仲夏。

我們的吟遊詩人撥銀弦名揚四方:
我們的青年比南國情郎更大膽:
我們的少女歡快起舞時最嬌美:
我們不缺歌兒和歡娛的管弦,
不缺甜美的回音和天空般清澈的水,
還有那抵禦酷熱的月桂花環。

To Autumn

O Autumn, laden with fruit, and stained
With the blood of the grape, pass not, but sit
Beneath my shady roof; there thou may'st rest,
And tune thy jolly voice to my fresh pipe;
And all the daughters of the year shall dance!
Sing now the lusty song of fruits and flowers.

'The narrow bud opens her beauties to
The sun, and love runs in her thrilling veins;
Blossoms hang round the brows of morning, and
Flourish down the bright cheek of modest eve,
Till clust'ring Summer breaks forth into singing,
And feather'd clouds strew flowers round her head.

'The spirits of the air live on the smells
Of fruit; and joy, with pinions light, roves round
The gardens, or sits singing in the trees.'
Thus sang the jolly Autumn as he sat;
Then rose, girded himself, and o'er the bleak
Hills fled from our sight; but left his golden load.

秋之詠

秋啊,你滿載果實,染著葡萄的
血色,別走,請到我陰涼的屋頂下
坐一坐;那裡你可以稍事休憩,
將歡樂的聲調調進我清新的蘆笛,
所有歲月的女兒會翩然起舞!
那時,請你唱果實與花朵的歡歌。

「細嫩的蓓蕾向太陽綻開嬌美,
愛在她那顫動的血管裡蕩漾;
鮮花環飾著黎明的眉宇,飄蕩著
垂掛到羞怯的黃昏那明亮的臉龐,
於是稠密的夏迸發出歌聲,
長翅的雲在她頭上灑滿花朵。

大氣中的精靈靠果實的芬芳生存;
而歡樂,則帶著有翼的光,繞花園
遊蕩,或者棲息在樹叢中歌唱。」
歡樂的秋坐著的時候,這樣唱著。
然後起身,整整衣裝,就越過蒼山
從視野中消失;但遺落了金色的擔子。

To Winter

'O Winter! bar thine adamantine doors:
The north is thine; there hast thou built thy dark
Deep-founded habitation. Shake not thy roofs,
Nor bend thy pillars with thine iron car.'

He hears me not, but o'er the yawning deep
Rides heavy; his storms are unchain'd, sheathed
In ribbed steel; I dare not lift mine eyes;
For he hath rear'd his sceptre o'er the world.

Lo! now the direful monster, whose skin clings
To his strong bones, strides o'er the groaning rocks:
He withers all in silence, and his hand
Unclothes the earth, and freezes up frail life.

He takes his seat upon the cliffs; the mariner
Cries in vain. Poor little wretch! that deal'st
With storms; till heaven smiles, and the monster
Is driv'n yelling to his caves beneath mount Hecla.

冬之詠

「冬啊！請將你剛硬的門閂緊：
北方屬於你；那裡你建起了黑暗、
幽深的寓所。別震顫你的屋頂，
不要用你的鐵戰車將柱子撞彎。」

他沒有理我，從天空的深淵上面
沉重地馳過；他的風暴被釋放——
包裹著鋼肋，我不敢抬起雙眼；
因為他向全世界高舉著權杖。

瞧！現在這可怕的魔怪，皮包著
粗大的骨骼，跨過呻吟的岩石：
使一切萎於死寂，用手剝盡
大地的綠衣，凍結了脆弱的生命。

他在海邊的峭壁上坐下；水手們
徒然地哭喊，渺小可憐的人們——
應付著風暴；直到天空笑，那魔怪
哭嚷著被趕進赫克勒山❶下的洞門。

---

❶火山，在冰島南部。

To the Evening Star

Thou fair-hair'd angel of the evening,
Now, whilst the sun rests on the mountains, light
Thy bright torch of love; thy radiant crown
Put on, and smile upon our evening bed!
Smile on our loves; and, while thou drawest the
Blue curtains of the sky, scatter thy silver dew
On every flower that shuts its sweet eyes
In timely sleep. Let thy west wind sleep on
The lake; speak silence with thy glimmering eyes,
And wash the dusk with silver. Soon, full soon,
Dost thou withdraw; then the wolf rages wide,
And the lion glares thro' the dun forest:
The fleeces of our flocks are cover'd with
Thy sacred dew: protect them with thine influence.

To Morning

O holy virgin! clad in purest white,
Unlock heav'n's golden gates, and issue forth;
Awake the dawn that sleeps in heaven; let light
Rise from the chambers of the east, and bring

晚星之詠

你金髮的黃昏之使啊,
此刻,太陽已安息在群山,請點燃
你輝煌的愛之火炬;戴上
你絢麗的花冠,向我們的臥床微笑!
請向我們的愛人微笑,當你拉開
天空那藍色的窗簾,請把銀露
灑遍每一朵花,它們在適時的夢中
已將甜美的眼睛合上。讓你的西風沉睡
在湖上;以閃爍的眼睛說出靜寂,
給暮色鍍上銀光。真快,那麼快,
你隱退了;於是狼到處狂嚎,
獅眼從幽暗的林中爍爍放光:
我們的羊群的絨毛,覆著你神聖的
清露:請以你的影響將它們呵護。

黎明之詠

神聖的處女啊!你披著最潔白的衣裳,
請打開天國的金色大門,走出來,
喚醒沉睡在天上的曙光;讓光明
從東方的寢宮升起;將甘甜清露

The honied dew that cometh on waking day.
O radiant morning, salute the sun,
Rouz'd like a huntsman to the chace; and, with
Thy buskin'd feet, appear upon our hills.

Fair Elenor

The bell struck one and shook the silent tower;
The graves give up their dead: fair Elenor
Walked by the castle gate, and looked in.
A hollow groan ran through the dreary vaults.

She shrieked aloud, and sunk upon the steps
On the cold stone her pale cheek. Sickly smells
Of death issue as from a sepulchre,
And all is silent but the sighing vaults.

Chille death withdraws his hand, and she revives;
Amazed, she finds herself upon her feet,
And, like a ghost, through narrow passages
Walking, feeling the cold walls with her hands.

隨甦醒的白晝一起,帶給人世。
絢麗的黎明啊,快去迎接問候那
如同待獵的獵人般被喚醒的太陽,
並邁著你穿厚靴的腳出現在山崗。

美麗的愛莉諾

鐘敲一點,震動了寂靜的城樓;
墳墓放出死者:美麗的愛莉諾
經過城堡的大門旁,向裡張望,
一聲陰沉的呻吟從墓穴中傳過。

她尖叫一聲,癱倒在石階上面。
蒼白的臉頰貼著冰冷的石板。
死神的噁心味飄來,猶自墓中,
一片死寂,惟有墓穴在悲嘆。

冰冷的死神縮回手,她甦醒過來,
驚奇地見到自己站立著,像幽靈
她用雙手摸索著冰冷的牆壁,
在狹窄的過道裡試探著緩緩前行。

Fancy returns, and now she thinks of bones,
And grinning skulls, and corruptible death,
Wrapped in his shroud; and now fancies she hears
Deep sighs and sees pale sickly ghosts gliding.

At length, no fancy, but reality
Distracts her. A rushing sound, and the feet
Of one that fled, approaches — Ellen stood,
Like a dumb statue, froze to stone with fear.

The wretch approaches, crying, 'The deed is done;
Take this, and send it by whom thou wilt send;
It is my life — send it to Elenor —
He's dead, and howling after me for blood!

'Take this,' he cried; and thrust into her arms
A wet napkin, wrapped about; then rushed
Past, howling: she received into her arms
Pale death and followed on the wings of fear.

They passed swift through the outer gate; the wretch,
Howling, leaped o'er the wall into the moat,
Stifling in mud. Fair Ellen passed the bridge,
And heard a gloomy voice cry, 'Is it done?'

幻覺又來了,迷幻中她想到了屍骨,
齜牙咧嘴的骷髏,和裹著屍衣的
易腐的屍首;迷幻中她聽到深深的
嘆息,看到蒼白的幽靈飄移。

終於,迷惑著她的不再是幻覺
而是真實,一種奔跑聲,一個人
逃竄的腳步聲近了——愛倫❷站著,
像靜默的雕像,凝在石頭上,恐懼萬分。

那歹徒近了,他喊著:「木已成舟了,
拿著它,派你願派的人把它送去,
它是我的命——把它送給愛莉諾:
他死了,跟在我後面嚎哭著索命!」

「拿著它,」他喊道;朝她胳膊裡
塞了塊裹著的濕頭巾,然後嚎哭著
奔了過去:她用胳膊挽住
蒼白的死神,跟著他;乘著恐怖之翼。

他們匆匆穿過外門;那歹徒
嚎哭著躍過牆頭,跳進護城溝,
悶死在泥淖裡,美麗的愛倫過橋後
聽見一聲陰沉的喊叫:「幹完了嗎?」

---
❷即愛莉諾。

As the deer wounded, Ellen flew over
The pathless plain; as the arrows that fly
By night, destruction flies and strikes in darkness.
She fled from fear, till at her house arrived.

Her maids await her; on her bed she falls,
That bed of joy, where erst her lord hath pressed:
'Ah, womans' fear!' she cried; 'Ah, cursed duke!
Ah, my dear lord! ah, wretched Elenor!

'My lord was like a flower upon the brows
Of lusty May! Ah, life as frail as flower!
O ghastly death, withdraw thy cruel hand,
Seek'st thou that flower to deck thy horrid temples?

'My lord was like a star in the highest heaven,
Drawn down to earth by spells and wickedness;
My lord was like the opening eyes of day,
When western winds creep softly o'er the flowers.

'But he is darkened; like the summer' noon,
Clouded; fallen like the stately tree cut down;
The breath of heaven dwelt among his leaves.
O Elenor, weak woman, filled with woe!'

Thus having spoke, she raised up her head,

像一隻受傷的鹿,愛倫飛過
荒蕪的平原;如同夜間的飛矢
毀滅在空中飛翔,在黑暗中襲擊,
到達家中後她才擺脫了恐懼。

她的侍女迎著她,她倒在床上,
那歡樂之床,她的夫君曾壓過:
「女人的恐懼啊!」她哭著:「該死的公爵!
我那親愛的夫君啊!不幸的愛莉諾!」

「我夫君曾像快樂五月的峭壁上
一朵花!生命就像花一樣脆弱!
可怕的死神,縮回你殘酷的手吧!
難道你要它打扮你可怕的鬢角?」

「我夫君曾像天頂上一顆星星,
卻被符咒和邪惡吸落到地上;
我夫君曾像黎明那初開的眼睛,
當那西風在花兒上飄移輕輕。」

「但他已黯淡:像夏日正午罩烏雲,
他已倒下,像高貴的大樹被砍倒;
天空的呼吸寓於他的綠葉中。
愛莉諾,柔弱的女人啊,充滿酸辛!」

這樣說完之後,她抬起頭來,

And saw the bloody napkin by her side,
Which in her arms she brought; and now, tenfold
More terrified, saw it unfold itself.

Her eyes were fixed; the bloody cloth unfolds,
Disclosing to her sight the murdered head
Of her dear lord, all ghastly pale, clotted
With gory blood; it groaned, and thus it spake:

'O Elenor, behold thy husband' head,
Who, sleeping on the stones of yonder tower,
Was reft of life by the accursed duke!
A hired villain turned my sleep to death.

'O Elenor, beware the cursed duke,
O give not him thy hand, now I am dead;
He seeks thy love — who, coward, in the night
Hired a villain to bereave my life.'

She sat with dead cold limbs, stiffened to stone;
She took the gory head up in her arms;
She kissed the pale lips; she had no tears to shed;
She hugged it to her breast, and groaned her last.

看著她身旁那塊染血的頭巾——
她用胳膊把它帶來，這時候
她萬分驚恐地看到它自動打開。

她眼睛直了；染血的頭巾打開後
眼前出現了她親愛的夫君的頭，
那被人割下的頭顱蒼白得可怕，
血跡斑斑；它呻吟著，這樣說道：

「愛莉諾啊，我是你的丈夫的頭，
他，睡在城樓的石頭上時，
被那可憎的公爵奪去了生命！
受雇的歹徒使我死在夢中！」

「愛莉諾啊，你要小心那該死的公爵；
我雖已死，你可千萬別答應他；
他追求你的愛，這個懦夫，在夜間
雇了個歹徒斷送了我的性命！」

她坐著，四肢冰涼，硬如石頭；
她用胳膊抱著血跡斑斑的頭；
她吻那蒼白的唇，欲哭無淚；
她把它緊抱在胸前，在嘆息中嚥氣。

Song

How sweet I roam'd from field to field,
  And tasted all the summer's pride,
'Till I the prince of love beheld,
  Who in the sunny beams did glide!

He shew'd me lilies for my hair,
  And blushing roses for my brow;
He led me through his gardens fair,
  Where all his golden pleasures grow.

With sweet May dews my wings were wet,
  And Phoebus fir'd my vocal rage;
He caught me in his silken net,
  And shut me in his golden cage.

He loves to sit and hear me sing,
  Then, laughing, sports and plays with me;
Then stretches out my golden wing,
  And mocks my loss of liberty.

歌：多麼快活

多麼快活，我漫遊四方。
　　將夏日的精華盡行品嘗，
直到我見到那愛的帝王，
　　在和煦的陽光中輕輕飄翔！

他用百合裝飾我頭髮，
　　用赧顏的玫瑰裝飾我的額；
他引我穿過他美麗的花園，
　　園中長滿他金色的歡樂。

五月的蜜露濕了我翅膀，
　　菲伯斯燃起我歌唱的激情；
他把我捉進柔絲的羅網，
　　用黃金的囚籠把我拘禁。

他愛坐著，聽我歌唱，
　　然後笑著，和我嬉戲；
再鋪開我的金色翅膀，
　　嘲笑我的自由的失去。

Song

My silks and fine array,
   My smiles and languish'd air,
By love are driv'n away;
   And mournful lean Despair
Brings me yew to deck my grave:
Such end true lovers have.

His face is fair as heav'n,
   When springing buds unfold;
O why to him was't giv'n,
   Whose heart is wintry cold?
His breast is love' all worship'd tomb,
Where all love's pilgrims come.

Bring me an axe and spade,
   Bring me a winding sheet;
When I my grave have made,
   Let winds and tempests beat:
Then down I'll lie, as cold as clay.
True love doth pass away!

歌：我的綢衣

我的綢衣與紅裝，
　我的微笑與慵懶，
都被愛情驅散；
　哀傷枯瘦的絕望
帶給我修飾墳墓的紫杉，
情真者就這樣終場。

他的臉天空般明朗——
　當萌動的花蕾開放；
他的心寒冬般冰冷——
　為何給他那臉龐？
他胸懷是愛所崇拜的墳墓，
愛的朝聖者都光顧。

請給我一輛斧一把鍬，
　請給我一件屍衣；
當我把墳墓掘好，
　請激盪起狂風暴雨：
我會躺下，冰冷如泥，
真誠的愛情才逝去！

Song

Love and harmony combine,
And around our souls intwine,
While thy branches mix with mine,
And our roots together join.

Joys upon our branches sit,
Chirping loud, and singing sweet;
Like gentle streams beneath our feet
Innocence and virtue meet.

Thou the golden fruit dost bear,
I am clad in flowers fair;
Thy sweet boughs perfume the air,
And the turtle buildeth there.

There she sits and feeds her young,
Sweet I hear her mournful song;
And thy lovely leaves among,
There is love: I hear his tongue.

There his charming nest doth lay,
There he sleeps the night away;

歌：愛情與和諧

愛情與和諧交融，
縈繞著我們的心靈，
當你我枝葉錯綜，
根與根也相連相並。

歡樂在我們的枝頭棲息，
鳴得響亮，唱得甜蜜；
像輕悠的流水在我們腳下，
天真與善美相聚在一起。

你有金色的果實累累，
我披一身美麗的花朵；
你的香枝使大氣芬芳，
還有海龜在那邊做窩。

那裡她孵卵和哺育幼仔，
聽她的哀歌我很愜意；
你的可愛的樹葉之中
有著愛情：我聽到他言語。

那裡他安著迷人的香巢，
用睡眠將黑夜打發過去；

There he sports along the day,
And doth among our branches play.

Song

I love the jocund dance,
  The softly-breathing song,
Where innocent eyes do glance,
  And where lisps the maiden's tongue.

I love the laughing vale,
  I love the echoing hill,
Where mirth does never fail,
  And the jolly swain laughs his fill.

I love the pleasant cot,
  I love the innocent bow'r,
Where white and brown is our lot,
  Or fruit in the mid-day hour.

I love the oaken seat,
  Beneath the oaken tree,
Where all the old villagers meet,
  And laugh our sports to see.

那裡他整天玩耍和嬉笑，
還在我們的樹枝間遊戲。

歌：我愛

我愛輕快歡樂的舞蹈，
　我愛輕柔生動的歌曲，
裡面有天真的眼睛忽閃，
　裡面有姑娘們咬舌私語。

我愛眉開眼笑的溪谷，
　我愛回音四起的山陵，
那裡有笑顏永不衰逝，
　快活的情人歡笑盡情。

我愛舒適宜人的茅廬，
　我愛快樂無憂的閨閣。
白色棕色是我們的園圃，
　也是中午時果子的光澤。

我愛那些橡木的座位，
　擺在那棵橡樹的下面，
村裡的老人都來聚會，
　笑呵呵看我們遊戲消遣。

I love our neighbors all,
    But, Kitty, I better love thee;
And love them I ever shall;
    But thou art all to me.

Song

Memory, hither come,
    And tune your merry notes;
And, while upon the wind
    Your music floats,
I'll pore upon the stream,
Where sighing lovers dream,
And fish for fancies as they pass
Within the watery glass.

I'll drink of the clear stream,
    And hear the linnet's song;
And there I'll lie and dream
    The day along:
And, when night comes, I'll go
    To places fit for woe;
Walking along the darken'd valley,
    With silent Melancholy.

我愛我們所有的鄰人,
　　但是吉蒂,我最愛你,
我將永遠地愛著他們,
　　但你是我的一切所寓。

歌:記憶,到這裡來

記憶,到這裡來
　　唱起你歡樂的歌曲;
而,當你的歌聲
　　乘著風兒飄去,
我將在流水旁沉思,
傍夢中嘆息的情侶,
我將在似水的明鏡中,
捕釣縹緲的幻夢。

我將飲清清的流水,
　　聽那紅雀的歌聲;
我將在那兒躺下,
　　整天整日地做夢;
夜來時,我將走向
　　宜於悲傷的地方,
沿黑暗的溪谷徒倚,
　　懷著沉默的憂鬱。

Mad Song

The wild winds weep,
   And the night is a-cold;
Come hither, Sleep,
   And my griefs infold:
But lo! the morning peeps
   Over the eastern steeps,
And the rustling birds of dawn
The earth do scorn.

Lo! to the vault
   Of paved heaven,
With sorrow fraught
   My notes are driven:
They strike the ear of night,
   Make weep the eyes of day;
They make mad the roaring winds,
   And with tempests play.

Like a fiend in a cloud
   With howling woe,
After night I do crowd,
   And with night will go;

瘋狂之歌

狂風淒厲地哭泣,
　夜冷得瑟瑟發抖;
到這裡來吧,睡神,
　來擁抱我的哀愁:
可是,瞧!在東方,
　晨光在峭壁上窺望,
晨鳥正颯颯地飛起,
　輕蔑地離開大地。

看,向烏雲
　密布的天穹,
充滿悲傷
　我的歌被驅送:
它震蕩著夜的耳朵,
　使白晝淚水盈眶;
它使呼嘯的風發狂,
　又將暴風雨嘲弄。

像陰影中的魔鬼,
　帶著極度悲淒,
我在夜來後聚起,
　還將隨夜同去;

I turn my back to the east,
From whence comforts have increas'd;
For light doth seize my brain
With frantic pain.

Song

Fresh from the dewy hill, the merry year
Smiles on my head, and mounts his flaming car;
Round my young brows the laurel wreathes a shade,
And rising glories beam around my head.

My feet are wing'd, while o'er the dewy lawn,
I meet my maiden, risen like the morn:
Oh bless those holy feet, like angels' feet;
Oh bless those limbs, beaming with heav'nly light!

Like as an angel glitt'ring in the sky,
In times of innocence and holy joy;
The joyful shepherd stops his grateful song,
To hear the music of an angel's tongue.

So when she speaks, the voice of Heaven I hear;
So when we walk, nothing impure comes near;

我向東方轉過去脊背，
避開那滋長著的安慰❸；
因為光將我大腦抓住，
用令人發狂的痛苦。

歌：從綴滿露珠的山崗

從綴滿露珠的山崗，歡樂的歲月明朗地
向我的頭顱微笑著，登上火的戰車；
圍著我年輕的眉宇，月桂葉綴成一圈，
繞著我的頭顱升起了榮光之環。

我雙足生翼，當在凝露的草坪對面
我遇見我的姑娘出現，像黎明一樣：
祝福啊，那聖潔的雙腳，宛如天使之足，
祝福啊，那皎皎的雙臂，放著天國之光！

彷彿，當一位天使在天空熠熠生輝，
在天真與神聖的歡樂所主的時代；
快樂的牧人停下了他歡樂的歌唱，
傾聽天使唇邊的仙樂，就那樣——

她一啓唇，我就聽到了天國的聲音；
我們漫步時，所有不潔的都不敢臨近；

---

❸可能指使魔鬼害怕的聖靈的「安慰」，comforts 有「聖靈」
之意。

Each field seems Eden, and each calm retreat;
Each village seems the haunt of holy feet.

But that sweet village where my black-ey'd maid
Closes her eyes in sleep beneath night's shade:
Whene'er I enter, more than mortal fire
Burns in my soul, and does my song inspire.

Song

When early morn walks forth in sober grey,
Then to my black ey'd maid I haste away;
When evening sits beneath her dusky bow'r,
And gently sighs away the silent hour,
The village bell alarms, away I go;
And the vale darkens at my pensive woe.

To that sweet village, where my black ey'd maid
Doth drop a tear beneath the silent shade,
I turn my eyes; and, pensive as I go,
Curse my black stars, and bless my pleasing woe.

Oft when the summer sleeps among the trees,
Whisp'ring faint murmurs to the scanty breeze,
I walk the village round; if at her side

每一片田野和每一處幽居,都像伊甸;
每一個村莊都似神靈常去的樂園。

而每當我來到那甜蜜可愛的村莊——
在那夜幕之下,我的黑眼睛的少女
合眼入睡的地方,就有非凡的火焰,
在我靈魂裡灼灼燃燒,將我的歌喚起。

歌:當晨曦

當晨曦穿著樸素的灰衣緩步前來,
我就匆匆離家去看我黑眼睛的姑娘;
當黃昏憩息在她幽暗的閨房下面,
輕輕嘆息著打發走寂靜的時光;
村裡的鐘聲響起,我就啟身離去,
溪谷因為我的憂鬱的悲傷而黯然。

向著那甜蜜的村莊,我的黑眼睛的姑娘,
在那寂靜的夜幕下滴落過淚珠的地方,
我回首矚望,我一邊走,一邊沉思著
咒我的黑星,祝福我的愉快的悲傷。

當夏在樹林中沉睡的時候,我常常
對著稀疏的微風含糊地喃喃低語著,
繞著村莊徘徊;如果有一個青年

A youth doth walk in stolen joy and pride,
I curse my stars in bitter grief and woe,
That made my love so high, and me so low.

O should she e'er prove false, his limbs I'd tear,
And throw all pity on the burning air;
I'd curse bright fortune for my mixed lot,
And then I'd die in peace, and be forgot.

To the Muses

Whether on Ida's shady brow,
   Or in the chambers of the East,
The chambers of the sun, that now
   From ancient melody have ceas'd;

Whether in Heav'n ye wander fair,
   Or the green corners of the earth,
Or the blue regions of the air,
   Where the melodious winds have birth;

Whether on chrystal rocks ye rove
   Beneath the bosom of the sea
Wand'ring in many a coral grove,

在那僭據的歡樂和驕傲中在她身邊，
我就在痛苦和酸悲中詛咒我的黑星，
它使我的愛如此高貴，使我如此低賤。

我要撕碎他的四肢啊，將憐憫盡行
拋給燃燒的大氣，要是她對我負心；
我要為我的亂運詛咒命運的寵兒，
隨後我將平靜地死去，被人們遺忘。

致繆斯

無論在艾達❹那多陰的山坡，
　還是在東方的寢宮——
那太陽的寢宮——那裡
　古老的歌兒已停息；

無論在你們徜徉的天國，
　無論在大地綠色的角落，
還是在藍色的氣層——
　那裡已出生了悅耳的風；

無論在大海的胸懷下，
　珊瑚叢中，那你們漫遊的
水晶一樣的岩石之上，

---

❹在小亞細亞，據希臘神話，諸神曾在此山觀看特洛伊戰爭。

Fair Nine, forsaking Poetry!

How have you left the ancient love
   That bards of old enjoy'd in you!
The languid strings do scarcely move!
   The sound is forc'd, the notes are few!

Gwin, King of Norway

Come, kings, and listen to my song,
   When Gwin, the son of Nore,
Over the nations of the north
   His cruel sceptre bore.

The nobles of the land did feed
   Upon the hungry poor;
They tear the poor man's lamb and drive
   The needy from their door.

'The land is desolate; our wives
   And children cry for bread;
Arise, and pull the tyrant down;
   Let Gwin be humbled.'

Gordred the giant roused himself

拋棄著詩歌啊，美麗的九個❺！

你們如何遺棄了古老的愛，
　　吟遊詩人因你們而享有的愛！
倦怠的弦絲幾乎不再顫移！
　　聲音壓抑，音調弱細！

圭恩，挪威王

來，國王們，來聽我的歌：
　　那時圭恩，挪的兒子，
在北方各個民族上空，
　　將殘酷的權杖揮動：

大陸上那些個高貴的人們，
　　靠飢餓的窮人養活；
他們撕食著窮人的麵包，
　　把苦人從門前趕跑！

土地荒蕪，我們的妻兒
　　為了麵包而哭泣；
起來，起來推翻暴君，
　　讓圭恩威風掃地。

巨人戈吉德在山洞裡面

❺九個繆斯女神。

Selected Poems of William Blake

From sleeping in his cave;
He shook the hills, and in the clouds
   The troubled banners wave.

Bneath them rolled, like tempests black,
   The numerous sons of blood,
Like lions' whelps, roaring abroad,
   Seeking their nightly food.

Down Bleron' hills they dreadful rush,
   Their cry ascends the clouds —
The trampling horse, and clanging arms
   Like rushing mighty floods.

Their wives and children, weeping loud,
   Follow in wild array,
Howling like ghosts, furious as wolves,
   In the bleak wintry day.

'Pull down the tyrant to the dust,
   Let Gwin be humbled,'
They cry, 'And let ten thousand lives
   Pay for the tyrant's head.'

From tower to tower the watchmen cry,
   'O Gwin, the son of Nore,

從睡夢之中醒來；
他搖撼著山崗，在雲中
　動亂的旗幟飄動。

旗幟下，像黑色的風暴，
　無數的熱血兒郎，
滾滾向前；如幼獅，遍地吼著
　尋找夜食一樣。

他們排山倒海地衝向前去，
　吶喊聲聲直沖雲霄；
嗒嗒的駿馬和鏗鏘的刀槍
　像洶湧的洪水一樣！

他們的妻兒，哭成一片
　紛亂地跟在後面，
像幽靈一樣嚎哭著，猶如
　隆冬的狼一樣狂怒。

「打倒暴君，打倒在塵埃，
　讓圭恩威風掃地，」
他們喊道：「捨千萬條生命
　將暴君的頭顱換取。」

從城堡到城堡，守衛者喊著：
　「圭恩啊，挪的兒子，

Arouse thyself! the nations, black
   Like clouds, come rolling o'er.

Gwin reared his shield, his palace shakes,
   His chiefs come rushing round;
Each, like an awful thunder cloud,
   With voice of solemn sound.

Like reared stones around a grave
   They stand around the King;
Then suddenly each seized his spear,
   And clashing steel does ring.

The husbandman does leave his plough,
   To wade through fields of gore;
The merchant binds his brows in steel
   And leaves the trading shore;

The shepherd leaves his mellow pipe
   And sounds the trumpet shrill;
The workman throws his hammer down
   To heave the bloody bill.

Like the tall ghost of Barraton,
   Who sports in stormy sky,
Gwin leads his host, as black as night

快醒醒，各民族人民，已如同
　　烏雲，漫天滾來了！」

圭恩舉起盾，他的宮殿晃著，
　　他的將領從四處奔來；
一個個，如同可怕的雷雲，
　　響著陰沉的聲音。

像墳墓周圍豎立的墓石，
　　他們簇擁著國王；
突然間一個個抓起長矛，
　　鋼鐵碰撞，鐺啷亂響。

農民丟下了他們的犁耙，
　　沖殺過血染的戰場；
商人用鋼索鏈住跳板，
　　離開了貿易海岸。

牧人放下他的妙笛，
　　吹起了尖利的號角；
工人拋掉他的錘子，
　　舉起了染血的鉤刀。

像暴風雨中遊戲於天空的
　　巴拉頓的高大鬼魂，
圭恩帶領著軍隊，像瘟疫

Selected Poems of William Blake

When pestilence does fly,
With horses and with chariots;
    And all his spearmen bold,
March to the sound of mournful song,
    Like clouds around him rolled.

Gwin lifts his hand; the nations halt;
    'Prepare for war,' he cries —
Gordred appears; his frowning brow
    Troubles our northern skies.

The armies stand, like balances
    Held in the Almighty's hand:
'Gwin, thou hast filled thy measure up,
    Thou'rt swept from out the land.'

And now the raging armies rushed,
    Like warring mighty seas;
The heavens are shook with roaring war,
    The dust ascends the skies!

Earth smokes with blood, and groans and shakes
    To drink her children's gore,
A sea of blood; nor can the eye
    See to the trembling shore.

飛散時的夜一樣陰沉。
馬蹄嗒嗒,戰車隆隆,所有
　他的勇敢的投槍手
如同翻滾在他周圍的烏雲
　向哀歌的海灣挺進。

各民族停下了,圭恩抬起手
「準備戰鬥!」他高喊──
戈吉德出現了,他緊鎖的眉
　將北方的天空擾亂。

兩軍停下了,像天平握在
　全能的上帝手裡;
「圭恩,你氣數已盡,你已被
　開除出這塊土地。」

狂怒的軍隊衝了上去,
　像廝殺的汪洋大海;
天國隨咆哮的戰爭而顫動,
　塵土揚到了空中!

大地吞吐著血氣,嘆息顫抖,
　吸她的孩子的鮮血──
一個血的海洋啊,一眼望不見
　它的顫抖的海岸線!

And on the verge of this wild sea
   Famine and death doth cry;
The cries of women and of babes
   Over the field doth fly.

The king is seen raging afar
   With all his men of might;
Like blazing comets, scattering death
   Through the red feverous night.

Beneath his arm like sheep they die,
   And groan upon the plain;
The battle faints, and bloody men
   Fight upon hills of slain.

Now death is sick, and riven men
   Labour and toil for life;
Steed rolls on steed, and shield on shield,
   Sunk in this sea of strife.

The god of war is drunk with blood,
   The earth doth faint and fail;
The stench of blood makes sick the heavens;
   Ghosts glut the throat of hell.

O what have kings to answer for

在這狂暴的海洋的邊緣，
　　飢餓和死神在哭喊；
女人和嬰兒哭叫的聲音
　　在戰場的上空飄蕩。

遠遠地可見，國王在狷獗，
　　帶著所有的強兵，
像閃光的彗星在播撒死亡，
　　撒遍火紅的黑夜。

他手下他們綿羊般地躺倒，
　　在原野上嘆息呻吟；
戰鬥減弱了，血污的士兵
　　在送死的山上廝拼。

死神膩了，沮喪的士兵
　　為生存而苦苦掙扎，
駿馬輾駿馬，盾牌捲盾牌，
　　沉入混戰的大海。

戰神已經喝足了鮮血；
　　大地衰弱又昏厥；
血臭使天空作嘔，鬼魂
　　塞滿了地獄的咽喉！

啊，國王拿什麼來回答，

Before that awful throne,
When thousand deaths for vengeance cry,
And ghosts accusing groan?

Like blazing comets in the sky
That shake the stars of light,
Which drop like fruit unto the earth,
Through the fierce burning night;

Like these did Gwin and Gordred meet,
And the first blow decides;
Down from the brow unto the breast
Gordred his head divides.

Gwin fell; the sons of Norway fled,
All that remained alive;
The rest did fill the vale of death;
For them the eagles strive.

The river Dorman rolled their blood
Into the northern sea,
Who mourned his sons, and overwhelmed
The pleasant south country.

在威嚴的寶座❻之前；
死者無數喊著要報仇，
　　鬼魂在嘆息詛咒！

他像天空上閃光的彗星，
　　搖曳著明亮的星光，
像果子一樣隕落到下界，
　　穿過狂燒的黑夜；

就這樣，圭恩與戈吉德相遇，
　　並定局於最初的一擊；
從額角開始直到胸口，
　　戈吉德劈開了他的頭！

圭恩倒下了，挪威人逃了，
　　所有還活著的挪威人；
其餘的填滿了死亡之谷，
　　兀鷹爭食著他們。

多曼河滾流著他們的鮮血，
　　流入了北方的海洋；
他哀悼他的子孫，淹沒了
　　舒適的南方之邦。

---

❻上帝的寶座。

Song by a Shepherd (c. 1787)

Welcome, stranger, to this place,
Where joy doth sit on every bough,
Paleness flies from every face;
We reap not what we do not sow.

Innocence doth like a rose
Bloom on every maiden's cheek;
Honour twines around her brows,
The jewel health adorns her neck.

Song by an Old Shepherd

When silver snow decks Sylvio's clothes
And jewel hangs at shepherd's nose,
We can abide life's pelting storm
That makes our limbs quake, if our hearts be warm.

Whilst Virtue is our walking-staff
And Truth a lantern to our path,
We can abide life's pelting storm
That makes our limbs quake, if our hearts be warm.

牧人之歌 (約1787年)

歡迎，陌生人，歡迎你來這裡，
這兒每根樹枝上都棲息著歡愉，
蒼白從每一張臉上倉惶飛走，
不是我們種的，我們不收。

天真就像一朵嬌嫩的玫瑰，
在每個少女的臉上欣欣開放；
光榮環繞在她的眉宇周圍，
寶石般的健康裝飾著她的頸項。

老牧人之歌

當銀色的雪花裝點著西爾娃的衣裳，
寶石懸掛在牧人的鼻樑上，
我們能頂住那使我們四肢發顫、
發抖的生命的暴風雨，若我們的心溫暖。

有了美德當我們走路的拐杖，
真理當我們照路的燈籠，
我們能頂住那使我們四肢發顫、
發抖的生命的暴風雨，若我們的心溫暖。

Blow, boisterous Wind, stern Winter frown,
Innocence is a winter' gown;
So clad, we'll abide life's pelting storm
That makes our limbs quake, if our hearts be warm.

吹吧,狂風,嚴厲的冬天的皺眉,
天真是一件禦寒的長袍,穿了它,
我們將頂住那使我們四肢發顫、
發抖的生命的暴風雨,若我們的心溫暖。

1789

Songs of Innocence

天眞之歌

William Blake, *For Children: The Gates of Paradise*, object 3, 1793

Introduction

Piping down the valleys wild
Piping songs of pleasant glee,
On a cloud I saw a child,
And he laughing said to me:

'Pipe a song about a Lamb.'
So I piped with merry cheer.
'Piper pipe that song again—'
So I piped, he wept to hear.

'Drop thy pipe thy happy pipe,
Sing thy songs of happy cheer.'
So I sung the same again
While he wept with joy to hear.

'Piper sit thee down and write
In a book that all may read—'
So he vanish'd from my sight.
And I pluck'd a hollow reed,

序詩

吹著笛兒,我走下野谷,
我歡樂的笛聲隨風輕飄。
我看見雲彩上有個小孩❶,
孩子他笑著,向我說道:

「吹個歌唱小羊羔的歌!」
我興高采烈地吹了一曲。
「再吹,再吹一次那歌兒!」
我又吹時他淌下了淚滴。

「放下笛兒,那快樂的笛兒,
唱吧,唱唱那快樂的小曲。」
於是我就唱,唱那首歌,
他聽著,淌下了喜悅的淚滴。

「吹笛的人,坐下來寫吧,
寫成一本書,大家都能看。」
他剛說完,便隱去了形象,
我折下一根空心的蘆管,

---

❶指耶穌。

And I made a rural pen,
And I stain'd the water clear,
And I wrote my happy songs
Every child may joy to hear.

The Shepherd

How sweet is the Shepherd's sweet lot,
From the morn to the evening he strays:
He shall follow his sheep all the day
And his tongue shall be filled with praise.

For he hears the lambs' innocent call,
And he hears the ewes' tender reply,
He is watchful while they are in peace,
For they know when their Shepherd is nigh.

The Echoing Green

The Sun does arise,
And make happy the skies.
The merry bells ring
To welcome the Spring.
The skylark and thrush,

用它做一支土造水筆，
在筆中注滿清清河水，
我用它寫下快樂的歌謠，
孩子們都能高興地聽到。

牧羊人

牧人的好運多麼美妙！
從早到晚他到處遊蕩；
他得整天跟隨著羊群，
他的口中要充滿頌揚──

他聽到羔羊天真地叫，
他聽到母羊纖柔地嚷；
他警覺著：牠們安然無憂──
因為知道牧人在近旁。

回音草坪

太陽升起，
使天空歡喜；
鐘聲歡鳴，
將春天歡迎；
雲雀和鶇鳥，

The birds of the bush,
Sing louder around,
To the bells' chearful sound.
While our sports shall be seen
On the Ecchoing Green.

Old John with white hair
Does laugh away care,
Sitting under the oak,
Among the old folk.
They laugh at our play,
And soon they all say,
'Such, such were the joys,
When we all girls & boys,
In our youth-time were seen,
On the Echoing Green.'

Till the little ones weary
No more can be merry.
The sun does descend,
And our sports have an end:
Round the laps of their mothers,
Many sisters and brothers,
Like birds in their nest,
Are ready for rest:
And sport no more seen,

灌木林中的小鳥，
到處高聲唱——
和著歡欣的鐘鳴；
我們就開始遊戲
在那回音草坪。

滿頭白髮的老約翰
無憂無慮地笑著，
坐在橡樹下面，
坐在老人們中間；
他們笑我們嬉鬧，
不久他們都說道：
「這樣，這樣作樂還是
當我們，全都年紀輕輕，
還是孩子時幹的事：
在這回音草坪。」

直到小傢伙們倦了，
再也提不起興致；
太陽也落山了，
遊戲才跟著完事。
媽媽們的裙兜周圍，
圍滿了兄弟姐妹；
像鳥兒回到了窩裡，
即將進入夢境；
看不到還有人遊戲

On the darkening Green.

The Lamb

Little Lamb who made thee?
 Dost thou know who made thee?
Gave thee life & bid thee feed
By the stream & o'er the mead;
Gave thee clothing of delight,
Softest clothing wooly bright;
Gave thee such a tender voice,
Making all the vales rejoice:
 Little Lamb who made thee?
 Dost thou know who made thee?

 Little Lamb I'll tell thee,
 Little Lamb I'll tell thee:
He is called by thy name,
For he calls himself a Lamb:
He is meek & he is mild,
He became a little child:
I a child & thou a lamb,
We are called by his name.
 Little Lamb God bless thee.
 Little Lamb God bless thee.

在那漸黑的草坪。

羔羊

　　小羊羔兒,誰造了你?
　　你可知道是誰造了你?
給了你生命,吩咐你吃草,
在流水旁邊,遍青青草地;
給了你人見人愛的衣裳,
茸茸的衣裳,鮮艷又柔軟;
給了你那麼柔和的聲音,
讓所有的溪谷聽了都喜歡?
　　小羊羔兒,誰造了你?
　　你可知道是誰造了你?

　　小羊羔兒,我來告訴你,
　　小羊羔兒,我來告訴你,
他的名字和你的一樣,
因為他叫自己羊羔兒;
他又柔順,他又溫和,
他變成了一個小小孩兒:
我是小孩兒,你是羊羔兒,
我們全都叫他的名兒。
　　小羊羔兒,上帝保佑你,
　　小羊羔兒,上帝保佑你。

The Little Black Boy

My mother bore me in the southern wild,
And I am black, but O! my soul is white.
White as an angel is the English child,
But I am black as if bereav'd of light.

My mother taught me underneath a tree
And sitting down before the heat of day,
She took me on her lap and kissed me,
And pointing to the east began to say:

'Look on the rising sun: there God does live
And gives his light, and gives his heat away.
And flowers and trees and beasts and men recieve
Comfort in morning, joy in the noon day.

'And we are put on earth a little space,
That we may learn to bear the beams of love,
And these black bodies and this sun-burnt face
Is but a cloud, and like a shady grove.

'For when our souls have learn'd the heat to bear
The cloud will vanish; we shall hear his voice,

黑人小孩

我媽媽生我在南方荒涼的地方,
我黑,可是啊!我的靈魂潔白;
白得像天使的是英國人的孩子,
可我黑,黑得好像失去了光彩。

在白晝的暑熱中,媽媽坐下來,
在一棵樹下,她諄諄教導我;
她把我抱在膝上,把我親吻,
她指著東方,開始對我訴說:

「看升起的太陽!那兒住著上帝,
祂放射出光明,放射出熱;
花草樹木、飛禽走獸和人們
清晨得安慰,正午時分得歡樂。」

「我們被安置在一塊小小的天地,
我們可學著感受愛的光輝;
而這黑黑的肢體,曬黑的面容,
只是一片雲,也像是多蔭的樹叢。」

「當我們的靈魂學會忍受暑熱,
那雲會消弭,祂將召喚我們:

Saying: 'Come out from the grove my love & care,
And round my golden tent like lambs rejoice.' "

Thus did my mother say and kissed me,
And thus I say to little English boy:
When I from black and he from white cloud free,
And round the tent of God like lambs we joy:

I'll shade him from the heat till he can bear
To lean in joy upon our father's knee.
And then I'll stand and stroke his silver hair,
And be like him and he will then love me.

The Blossom

Merry Merry Sparrow
Under leaves so green
A happy Blossom
Sees you swift as arrow
Seek your cradle narrow
Near my Bosom.

『走出樹林來吧，我的愛和擔憂，
羔羊般快樂地圍著我金色的帳篷。』」

媽媽親著我，對我說了這些話。
我便這樣對英國人的孩子談講：
當我從黑雲❷、他從白雲❸得到解放，
羔羊般快樂地圍著上帝的篷帳，

我會為他遮蔭，到他能忍受熱，
能夠快樂地倚著父親❹的膝蓋；
我將站著，撫摸著他的銀髮，
變得像他一樣，得到他的愛。

鮮花

歡樂的歡樂的小雀，
在那麼綠的葉子下面，
一朵幸福的花兒
見到你箭一樣迅捷
尋找你狹小的巢穴
靠近我的心兒。

---

❷❸均指軀體。

❹上帝。

Pretty Pretty Robin
Under leaves so green
A happy Blossom
Hears you sobbing sobbing
Pretty Pretty Robin
Near my Bosom.

The Chimney Sweeper

When my mother died I was very young,
And my father sold me while yet my tongue
Could scarcely cry 'weep, 'weep, 'weep, 'weep.
So your chimneys I sweep & in soot I sleep.

There's little Tom Dacre, who cried when his head
That curl'd like a lamb's back, was shav'd, so I said,
'Hush Tom never mind it, for when your head's bare,
You know that the soot cannot spoil your white hair.'

And so he was quiet, & that very night,
As Tom was a sleeping he had such a sight,
That thousands of sweepers Dick, Joe, Ned & Jack
Were all of them lock'd up in coffins of black.

And by came an Angel who had a bright key,

美麗的美麗的歐鴿,
在那麼綠的葉子下面,
一朵幸福的花兒
聽到你啜泣,啜泣,
美麗的美麗的歐鴿。
靠近我的心兒。

掃煙囪的孩子

我媽死去的時候我還很小,
我爸賣了我,那時我的小嘴
還叫不出「掃,掃,掃,掃」,
於是你的煙囪我掃,煙灰裡我睡著。

有個小湯姆長著羊毛般的鬆髮,
剃光頭時他哭得傷心,我就對他說:
「噓,別介意,湯姆,光著頭知道
煙灰糟蹋不了你淡色的頭髮啦。」

他安靜了下來。就在那天夜裡,
湯姆在夢中見到這樣的景象:
掃煙囪的孩子迪克、喬、小凱……
千萬個全被關進黑洞洞的棺材。

後來,來了個帶著亮鑰匙的天使,

And he open'd the coffins & set them all free.
Then down a green plain leaping laughing they run
And wash in a river and shine in the Sun.

Then naked & white, all their bags left behind,
They rise upon clouds, and sport in the wind.
And the Angel told Tom if he'd be a good boy,
He'd have God for his father & never want joy.

And so Tom awoke and we rose in the dark
And got with our bags & our brushes to work.
Tho' the morning was cold, Tom was happy & warm,
So if all do their duty, they need not fear harm.

The Little Boy Lost

'Father, father, where are you going
O do not walk so fast.
Speak father, speak to your little boy
Or else I shall be lost.'

The night was dark, no father was there.
The child was wet with dew.
The mire was deep, & the child did weep
And away the vapour flew.

他打開棺材,讓他們自由地離去,
他們穿過原野,跳呀,笑呀,
在清清河水中洗澡,在陽光中沐浴。

再光著白淨的身子,扔了煙灰袋,
升上雲端,在風中追逐遊戲;
天使告訴湯姆,只要是好孩子,
就會有上帝做父親,再不缺歡娛。

湯姆醒了;我們在黑暗中起身,
背著煙灰袋,拿起掃帚去幹活,
早晨雖冷,湯姆卻又暖和又愉快,
所以盡本分了,就不必怕受到傷害。

男童之失

「爸爸,爸爸,你去哪兒呀?
你別走這麼快啊。
講話呀爸爸,和你的兒講話,
要不我會迷失啦。」

天黑了,哪裡有什麼爸爸;
孩子被露水沾濕了;
泥濘很深,孩子哭起來,
幻象也跟著消失了。

The Little Boy Found

The little boy lost in the lonely fen,
Led by the wand'ring light,
Began to cry, but God ever nigh,
Appeard like his father in white.

He kissed the child & by the hand led
And to his mother brought,
Who in sorrow pale, thro' the lonely dale
Her little boy weeping sought.

Laughing Song

When the green woods laugh with the voice of joy
And the dimpling stream runs laughing by,
When the air does laugh with our merry wit,
And the green hill laughs with the noise of it.

When the meadows laugh with lively green
And the grasshopper laughs in the merry scene,
When Mary and Susan and Emily,
With their sweet round mouths sing Ha, Ha, He.

男童之得

小男孩迷失在孤寂的沼澤裡,
向搖曳的燈光走去,
他哭著:但永在的上帝出現了,
像父親,穿著白衣。

他吻了孩子,攬著他的手, 5
帶領他去媽媽那裡:
她正愁苦地,在孤寂的山谷中
哭泣著找她的孩子。

笑歌

當綠色的樹林以歡快的聲音笑著,
那微波蕩漾的流水笑著跑過,
當大氣以我們的歡聲笑語笑著,
那綠色的山崗以它的喧聲笑著,

當草地以它生動的綠色笑著, 5
蚱蜢在那歡樂的景象中笑著,
當瑪麗,蘇珊,還有愛彌麗她們
以甜蜜的小嘴唱著:「哈哈——呵!」

When the painted birds laugh in the shade
Where our table with cherries and nuts is spread
Come live & be merry and join with me,
To sing the sweet chorus of Ha, Ha, He.

A Cradle Song

Sweet dreams form a shade,
O'er my lovely infant's head.
Sweet dreams of pleasant streams,
By happy silent moony beams.

Sweet sleep with soft down,
Weave thy brows an infant crown.
Sweet sleep Angel mild,
Hover o'er my happy child.

Sweet smiles in the night,
Hover over my delight.
Sweet smiles, Mother's smiles,
All the livelong night beguiles.

當色彩瑰麗的鳥兒在林蔭中笑著，
放著櫻桃和栗子的餐桌已擺開，
來住下吧，高高興興，和我一塊兒，
齊聲歡唱那悅耳的：「哈哈——呵！」

搖籃曲

甜蜜的夢兒，成一片暗影
罩在我可愛的嬰兒頭頂；
甜蜜地夢見怡人的流水，
借著幸福的靜月的光輝。

甜蜜的睡眠，用柔軟的絨羽，
將你❺的眉編織成童稚花冠。
甜蜜的睡眠啊溫柔的天使，
在幸福的孩兒上空盤旋。

甜蜜的微笑，在這夜間
在我的歡樂❻之上空盤旋；
甜蜜的微笑啊母親的微笑，
哄走整個漫長的夜晚。

---

❺指嬰兒。
❻指「你」——嬰兒。

Sweet moans, dove-like sighs,
Chase not slumber from thy eyes.
Sweet moans, sweeter smiles,
All the dovelike moans beguiles.

Sleep sleep happy child.
All creation slept and smil'd.
Sleep sleep, happy sleep,
While o'er thee thy mother weep.

Sweet babe in thy face,
Holy image I can trace.
Sweet babe once like thee,
Thy maker lay and wept for me,

Wept for me, for thee, for all,
When he was an infant small.
Thou his image ever see,
Heavenly face that smiles on thee;

Smiles on thee, on me, on all,
Who become an infant small,
Infant smiles are his own smiles,
Heaven & earth to peace beguiles.

甜蜜的呻吟和溫柔的嘆息
不會驅走你眼中的睡意。
甜蜜的呻吟和更甜的微笑
哄走所有溫柔的囈語。

睡吧，睡吧，幸福的孩子，
天地萬物已微笑著安息；
睡吧，睡吧，幸福的睡吧，
俯望著你，媽媽在哭泣。

甜蜜的寶貝，在你臉上
我能看到神聖的形象。
甜蜜的寶貝，曾經像你
造你者躺著，為我哭訴。

為我哭泣，為你，為全體，
那時他還是個小小的幼嬰，
你永遠看見他的形象——
超凡的面容微笑吟吟。

向你微笑，向我，向全體，
他變成過一個小小的幼嬰，
童稚的微笑是他的真容，
將天國和塵世哄慰入靜。

The Divine Image

To Mercy Pity Peace and Love,
All pray in their distress:
And to these virtues of delight
Return their thankfulness.

For Mercy Pity Peace and Love
Is God our father dear:
And Mercy Pity Peace and Love
Is Man his child and care.

For Mercy has a human heart
Pity, a human face,
And Love, the human form divine,
And Peace, the human dress.

Then every man of every clime,
That prays in his distress,
Prays to the human form divine
Love Mercy Pity Peace.

And all must love the human form,
In heathen, turk or jew.

至上的形象

向仁慈、和平、憐憫與愛，
所有憂傷者懇切祈禱：
對這些蘊含著歡樂的美德，
他們以感激予以回報。

因仁慈、和平、憐憫與愛，
是上帝，我們親愛的父：
仁慈、和平、憐憫與愛，
也是人——他的孩子和關注。

因為仁慈有一顆人心，
憐憫，有一張人的臉龐；
愛，有著至上的人形，
和平，有一套人的服裝。

所以每一塊地方每一個
處於憂傷之中的祈禱者，
都向至上的人形祈求
愛與仁慈與憐憫與和平。

所有人都得愛人的形象，
愛猶太人，土耳其人，土著，

Where Mercy, Love & Pity dwell
There God is dwelling too.

Holy Thursday

'Twas on a Holy Thursday, their innocent faces clean,
The children walking two & two in red & blue & green;
Grey headed beadles walkd before with wands as white as snow,
Till into the high dome of Paul's they like Thames' waters flow.

O what a multitude they seemed, these flowers of London town;
Seated in companies they sit with radiance all their own.
The hum of multitudes was there but multitudes of lambs,
Thousands of little boys and girls raising their innocent hands.

Now like a mighty wind they raise to heaven the voice of song
Or like harmonious thunderings the seats of heaven among.
Beneath them sit the aged men, wise guardians of the poor.
Then cherish pity, lest you drive an angel from your door.

Night

The sun descending in the west,
The evening star does shine.

它寓有仁慈與愛與憐憫，
上帝也在其中居住。

升天節

升天節到了，天真的臉蛋洗得乾乾淨淨，
孩子們一對對走著，穿著紅黃綠各色衣裙，
灰髮的助理牧師在前，執著雪一樣白的手杖，
像泰晤士河水一樣，他們流進了保羅大廳。

這麼一大群孩子啊！這些倫敦市的花朵！
他們神采奕奕，自動地結伴坐在一起，
一大群響著嗡嗡的聲音，只是一大群羔羊啊，
無數男孩和女孩，舉起了天真的手臂。

他們向天國揚起的歌聲，就像勁風一樣，
宛若天國的席位間悅耳的雷聲飛馳。
他們後面是成年人——窮人賢明的保護者；
此刻你要心懷憐憫：免得從門前趕走天使。

夜

夕陽沉落西山，
晚星閃耀在天上，

The birds are silent in their nest,
And I must seek for mine.
The moon, like a flower,
In heaven's high bower,
With silent delight
Sits and smiles on the night.

Farewell green fields and happy groves,
Where flocks have took delight;
Where lambs have nibbled, silent moves
The feet of angels bright;
Unseen they pour blessing,
And joy without ceasing,
On each bud and blossom,
And each sleeping bosom.

They look in every thoughtless nest,
Where birds are covered warm;
They visit caves of every beast,
To keep them all from harm.
If they see any weeping,
That should have been sleeping,
They pour sleep on their head
And sit down by their bed.

When wolves and tygers howl for prey

鳥兒在巢中安眠，
我也要將我的巢尋訪。
月亮，像一朵花兒，
靜靜地懷著喜悅；
它安憩在高高的天庭，
對夜微笑吟吟。

別了啊，碧野和綠林，
這兒曾有欣欣
羊群，羔羊啃青，
歡快的天使腳步輕盈。
她們將歡樂和祝福
無形地不斷傾注
在每朵鮮花和蓓蕾上，
在所有沉睡的胸上。

她們探遍不慎的鳥巢，
把鳥兒蓋得和和暖暖，
她們訪遍動物的洞穴，
使他們不受傷殘；
她們若見誰哭泣，
誰就會熟睡過去──
灑睡眠於他們頭上，
還坐在他們身旁。

當虎狼發出捕食的吼聲，

They pitying stand and weep;
Seeking to drive their thirst away,
And keep them from the sheep.
But if they rush dreadful;
The angels most heedful,
Recieve each mild spirit,
New worlds to inherit.

And there the lion's ruddy eyes
Shall flow with tears of gold:
And pitying the tender cries,
And walking round the fold:
Saying: "Wrath by his meekness,
And by his health, sickness
Is driven away
From our immortal day.

'And now beside thee bleating lamb,
I can lie down and sleep;
Or think on him who bore thy name,
Grase after thee and weep.
For wash'd in life's river,
My bright mane forever
Shall shine like the gold,
As I guard o'er the fold.'

她們就站住,哀然而泣——
試圖驅散他們的渴望,
使他們免害群羊;
但他們若可怕地衝過去,
天使們就小心翼翼
接受每一個靈魂
去將新世界承繼。

那裡獅子紅色的眼睛
將會流出金色的淚:
並憐憫那些纖弱的呼叫,
漫步在羊群周圍
說道:「狂怒,被他的
柔順;疾病,被他的
健康,驅逐出了
我們的永恆之世。」

「在你身旁,咩咩的羔羊啊,
我現在能夠躺下睡去;
或想著有你名字的他,
在後面吃草和哭泣——
經過生命河的洗禮,
我的閃亮的鬃毛
將永遠閃耀如金,
當我守護著羊群。」

Spring

Sound the Flute!
Now it' mute.
Birds delight
Day and Night.
Nightingale
In the dale
Lark in Sky
Merrily
Merrily Merrily to welcome in the Year.

Little Boy
Full of joy.
Little Girl
Sweet and small,
Cock does crow
So do you.
Merry voice
Infant noise
Merrily Merrily to welcome in the Year.

Little Lamb
Here I am.

春

　　吹起長笛！
　　正當沉寂。
　　鳥兒嬉鬧
　　白天夜裡；
　　夜鶯夜鶯
　　溪谷中鳴，
　　雲雀凌空，
　　歡樂地，
歡樂地，歡樂地，迎接新年。

　　小男孩兒
　　歡天喜地，
　　小女孩兒
　　可愛伶俐，
　　雄雞歡叫，
　　你也歡叫；
　　歡樂之聲，
　　童之喧聲，
歡樂地，歡樂地，迎接新年。

　　小羔羊兒，
　　我在這兒，

Come and lick

My white neck.

Let me pull

Your soft Wool.

Let me kiss

Your soft face.

Merrily Merrily we welcome in the Year.

Nurse's Song

When the voices of children are heard on the green

And laughing is heard on the hill,

My heart is at rest within my breast

And every thing else is still.

'Then come home my children, the sun is gone down

And the dews of night arise;

Come come leave off play, and let us away

Till the morning appears in the skies.'

'No no let us play, for it is yet day

And we cannot go to sleep;

Besides in the sky, the little birds fly

And the hills are all covered with sheep.'

過來舔舔
我雪白的脖兒,
讓我拉拉
你柔軟的毛兒,
讓我親親
你柔軟的臉兒,
歡樂地,歡樂地,迎接新年。

保母之歌

當孩子們的聲音從草坪傳來,
歡笑聲聲飄蕩在山崗,
我的心中就一片安寧,
周身都覺得寧靜安詳。

「該回來了,我的孩子,太陽下山了,
夜間的露水也已經出來;
得了,得了,快走吧,別玩了,
到明天天亮再來。」

「不,不,讓我們玩嘛,還是白天哪,
我們一點也不想上床;
還有,小鳥兒還在天上飛翔,
滿山遍野佈滿了綿羊。」

'Well well go & play till the light fades away
And then go home to bed.'
The little ones leaped & shouted & laugh'd
And all the hills ecchoed.

Infant Joy

'I have no name
I am but two days old.'
What shall I call thee?"
'I happy am
Joy is my name.'
Sweet Joy befall thee!

Pretty joy!
Sweet joy but two days old.
Sweet joy I call thee:
Thou dost smile.
I sing the while
Sweet joy befall thee!

A Dream

Once a dream did weave a shade,

「唉,唉,去玩吧,玩到看不見了,
你們再回家睡覺去。」
小孩們跳啊,叫啊,笑啊,
山丘間回音四起。

童稚的歡樂

「我沒有姓名:
出生只有兩天。」
那我怎麼叫你?
「我幸福歡欣,
歡樂是我的名。」
甜蜜的歡樂降給你!

美妙的歡樂!
甜蜜的歡樂才兩天,
「甜蜜的歡樂,」我稱你:
你甜甜地笑了,
我歌唱那一刻:
當甜蜜的歡樂降給你!

一個夢

曾有一個夢編著樹蔭,

O'er my Angel-guarded bed,
That an Emmet lost its way
Where on grass methought I lay.

Troubled, wilderd, and folorn;
Dark, benighted, travel-worn,
Over many a tangled spray
All heart-broke I heard her say:

'O my children! do they cry?
Do they hear their father sigh?
Now they look abroad to see,
Now return and weep for me.'

Pitying I dropp'd a tear;
But I saw a glow-worm near,
Who replied: "What wailing wight
Calls the watchman of the night?

'I am set to light the ground,
While the beetle goes his round;
Follow now the beetle's hum,
Little wanderer, hie thee home.'

在我那天使守護的床頂,
我看見一隻迷路的螞蟻,
覺得自己躺在草地。

(她)苦惱,困惑,又孤淒。
夜色昏黑,她力盡精疲,
(她)翻過許多糾結的草莖,
我聽到她心膽俱裂的聲音:

「我的孩子啊!他們在哭泣?
他們可聽到父親在嘆息?
他們一定四處去找我,
然後回去,為我哭泣。」

我流下了眼淚,為她哀慟;
但突然看到了一隻螢火蟲。
他應道:「是誰在哀哀地哭著
哀哀地呼喚夜的巡察者?」

「我是被派來照亮地面的,
還有甲蟲在到處巡察;
好了,循著甲蟲的聲音,
小小迷徒,趕緊回家。」

On Another's Sorrow

Can I see another's woe,
And not be in sorrow too?
Can I see another's grief,
And not seek for kind relief?

Can I see a falling tear,
And not feel my sorrow's share?
Can a father see his child
Weep, nor be with sorrow fill'd?

Can a mother sit and hear
An infant groan, an infant fear?
No no never can it be.
Never never can it be.

And can he who smiles on all
Hear the wren with sorrows small,
Hear the small bird's grief & care
Hear the woes that infants bear—

對別人的悲傷

我會見到別人的苦惱
而不隨之陷入傷悲？
我會見到別人的不幸
不為之尋求親切的安慰？

我會見到滴落的淚珠
不感到在將悲傷分擔？
會有父親看到孩子
哭泣，不充滿悲戚之感？

難道會有母親坐視著
嬰兒發出恐懼的呻吟？
不，不！永遠不會，
永遠，永遠不會。

對一切都微笑的他❼難道
會聽到鷦鷯有一絲悲傷，
聽到小鳥有不幸和煩惱，
聽到嬰兒忍受著苦惱，

---

❼指耶穌。耶穌投胎於聖母瑪麗亞腹內，變成了嬰兒。

And not sit beside the nest
Pouring pity in their breast,
And not sit the cradle near
Weeping tear on infant's tear?

And not sit both night & day,
Wiping all our tears away?
O! no never can it be.
Never never can it be.

He doth give his joy to all.
He becomes an infant small.
He becomes a man of woe.
He doth feel the sorrow too.

Think not, thou canst sigh a sigh,
And thy maker is not by.
Think not, thou canst weep a tear,
And thy maker is not near.

O! he gives to us his joy,
That our grief he may destroy;

而不坐在鳥巢旁邊,
傾注同情於牠們心裡;
而不坐在搖籃旁邊,
和嬰兒眼淚流在一起;

而不日日夜夜地坐著,
將我們的眼淚全都擦去?
啊,不!永遠不會。
永遠,永遠不會。

他將歡樂分給了全體,
他變成了一個小小的嬰孩,
他變成了一個有苦惱的人,
他也感到了憂傷和悲哀。

別以為你有一次嘆息
造物主他會不在前後,
別以為你有一次流淚
造物主他會不在左右。

啊!他❽給了我們愉悦,
我們的悲傷他會消滅;

---

❽指造物主——上帝,與前面的「他」——耶穌並不矛盾,按「三位一體」之說,上帝為聖父,耶穌為聖子,為一體。

Till our grief is fled and gone
He doth sit by us and moan.

他總是坐在一旁嘆息,
直等到我們的不幸離去。

1794

Songs of Experience

經驗之歌

William Blake, *For Children: The Gates of Paradise*, object 10, 1793

Introduction

Hear the voice of the Bard!
Who Present, Past, & Future sees,
Whose ears have heard
The Holy Word,
That walk'd among the ancient trees.

Calling the lapsed Soul
And weeping in the evening dew:
That might controll
The starry pole:
And fallen fallen light renew!

'O Earth O Earth return!
Arise from out the dewy grass;
Night is worn,
And the morn
Rises from the slumberous mass.

'Turn away no more:
Why wilt thou turn away?
The starry floor,
The watry shore

序詩

聽吟遊詩人之聲！
他看到現在、未來和過去，
他已聽見
神明之言
漫步在古老的樹林子裡。

呼喚迷失的靈魂
哭泣而涕下夜間的露水：
或許會操縱
北極明星
重新射出泯滅的光輝！

「地母啊，重現吧，地母！
請從露濕的草地上升起；
夜已消盡，
而那黎明
已從昏睡的一群中升起。」

「別再背轉你的臉：
你為何還要把臉背過去？
星照的地面，
潮濕的海岸

Is giv'n thee till the break of day.'

Earth's Answer

E arth rais'd up her head,
From the darkness dread & drear.
Her light fled:
Stony dread!
And her locks cover'd with grey despair.

'Prison'd on watry shore
Starry Jealousy does keep my den
Cold and hoar
Weeping o'er
I hear the Father of the ancient men.

'Selfish father of men!
Cruel, jealous, selfish fear!
Can delight
Chain'd in night
The virgins of youth and morning bear?

'Does spring hide its joy

在破曉之前一直付予你。」

大地的回答

地母抬起了她的頭,
從可怕而陰鬱的黑暗之上。
她的光逃隱:
恐怖得寒心!
她的頭髮上是灰色的絕望。

「我囚於潮濕的海岸,
繁星的嫉妒使我的臟巢
寒冷又霉爛,
我淚水哭乾
才聽到古人的父親❶來到,」

「因自私而善妒,膽怯!
這個人類的自私的父親喲!
你用黑夜
鏈住歡悅,
少女和黎明怎能忍受?」

「春天藏起了歡樂嗎,

---

❶指上帝。

When buds and blossoms grow?
Does the sower
Sow by night?
Or the plowman in darkness plow?

"Break this heavy chain,
That does freeze my bones around
Selfish! vain!
Eternal bane!
That free Love with bondage bound."

The Clod and the Pebble

'Love seeketh not Itself to please,
Nor for itself hath any care;
But for another gives its ease,
And builds a Heaven in Hell's despair.'

So sang a little Clod of Clay,
Trodden with the cattle's feet:
But a Pebble of the brook,
Warbled out these metres meet:

'Love seeketh only Self to please,
To bind another to its delight;

在蓓蕾和鮮花生長的時候？
播種者在夜間
播種的嗎？
耕犁者在暗中耕犁嗎？」

「砸碎這沉重的鎖鏈！
它僵住了我周身的筋骨，
自私！愚蠢！
永恒的毒根！
用奴役把自由的愛細住。」

土塊和卵石

「愛不圖自己滿意歡喜，
也不為自己小心留意，
卻為了他人獻出安逸，
在地獄的絕望中將天堂建起。」

一個小土塊這樣唱著，
被黏在牛腳上踏著踩著，
與一塊溪中的卵石相遇，
它婉轉地唱出這些韻律：

「愛只圖自己滿意歡喜，
強求於別人自己愜意，

Joys in another's loss of ease,
And builds a Hell in Heaven's despite.'

Holy Thursday

Is this a holy thing to see,
In a rich and fruitful land,
Babes reduced to misery,
Fed with cold and usurious hand?

Is that trembling cry a song?
Can it be a song of joy?
And so many children poor?
It is a land of poverty!

And their sun does never shine.
And their fields are bleak & bare.
And their ways are fill'd with thorns.
It is eternal winter there.

For where-e'er the sun does shine,
And where-e'er the rain does fall:
Babe can never hunger there,
Nor poverty the mind appall.

取樂於他人失去安逸,
在天堂的憎惡中將地獄建起。」

升天節

難道這能算是至善——
在富饒多產的土地上,
看見嬰兒的境遇悲慘,
被冰冷的放債的手撫養?

那嘶哭能算是歌聲?
能算是歡樂的歌曲?
那麼多孩子不幸啊,
那是塊貧瘠的土地!

那裡見不著陽光,
土地荒蕪不毛。
道路為荊棘所網,
冰雪四季不消。

哪裡有了陽光,
哪裡有雨露滋潤:
嬰兒就不會挨餓,
就不會有威嚇人的貧困。

The Little Girl Lost

In futurity
I prophetic see,
That the earth from sleep,
(Grave the sentence deep)

Shall arise and seek
For her maker meek:
And the desert wild
Become a garden mild.

In the southern clime,
Where the summer's prime,
Never fades away,
Lovely Lyca lay.

Seven summers old
Lovely Lyca told;
She had wanderd long,
Hearing wild birds' song.

'Sweet sleep come to me
Underneath this tree;

幼女之失

我預見
未來的大地,
將從睡夢中
(請深深銘記)

起來和尋覓
她溫順的造物主;
荒原將變為
和暖的花園。

在那南國之疆,
那夏日之精華
永不凋謝的地方,
躺著可愛的麗卡。

我們可愛的麗卡,
好像已經過七夏;
她聽著野鳥歌唱,
迷失的時間已很長。

「美麗的夢,快來吧,
我在這棵樹的下面,

Do father, mother weep —
'Where can Lyca sleep?'

'Lost in desert wild
Is your little child.
How can Lyca sleep,
If her mother weep?

'If her heart does ache,
Then let Lyca wake:
If my mother sleep,
Lyca shall not weep.

'Frowning frowning night,
O'er this desert bright,
Let thy moon arise,
While I close my eyes.'

Sleeping Lyca lay:
While the beasts of prey,
Come from caverns deep,
View'd the maid asleep.

The kingly lion stood
And the virgin view'd,
Then he gambold round

爸爸媽媽在哭嗎——
哪兒麗卡能成眠？」

「你們幼小的孩兒
已在荒原裡迷路。
麗卡怎麼能睡呢，
要是她媽媽在哭？」

「要是媽的心在作痛，
就讓麗卡醒著；
要是媽媽已安睡，
就不要讓麗卡傷悲。」

「愁眉不展的夜啊，
快升起你的月吧，
在這莽莽荒原，
當我合上雙眼。」

麗卡躺下睡了，
尋食的野獸來了；
從深深的大洞出來，
見到夢中的女孩。

那為王的獅子站立
朝那處女看著；
然後來回地轉，

O'er the hallowed ground:

Leopards, tygers play,
Round her as she lay;
While the lion old,
Bow'd his mane of gold.

And her bosom lick,
And upon her neck,
From his eyes of flame,
Ruby tears there came:

While the lioness
Loss'd her slender dress,
And naked they convey'd
To caves the sleeping maid.

The Little Girl Found

All the night in woe
Lyca's parents go:
Over vallies deep,
While the deserts weep.

Tired and woe-begone,

在那片聖地上跳著:

虎豹圍著她嬉戲,
學她躺著的姿勢,
而那年老的獅子,
垂下金燦燦的鬃絲。

他的火眼含淚,
他舔著她的胸脯,
他的寶石般的淚水,
落在她的頸部:

於是那些獅子
為她解開了薄衣,
裸著的少女在
沈睡中被抬往洞裡。

幼女之得

麗卡的父親和母親,
整夜地悲痛傷心:
尋遍了深深的山谷,
荒野為他們悲哭。

他們疲憊又愁悶,

Hoarse with making moan:
Arm in arm seven days,
They trac'd the desert ways.

Seven nights they sleep,
Among shadows deep:
And dream they see their child
Starv'd in desert wild.

Pale thro' pathless ways
The fancied image strays,
Famish'd, weeping, weak
With hollow piteous shriek.

Rising from unrest,
The trembling woman prest
With feet of weary woe;
She could no further go.

In his arms he bore
Her arm'd with sorrow sore;
Till before their way,
A couching lion lay.

Turning back was vain,
Soon his heavy mane,

呻吟得啞了嗓門：
他們相依為命地
在荒原裡摸索了七日。

七夜他們都睡在
濃濃的樹蔭裡面：
夢見他們的女孩
餓死在荒原中間。

夢見她邊哭邊走，
在荒野中迷失了方向，
虛弱加上飢餓，
哭聲嘶啞而淒涼。

睡不安只得起身，
那婦人直打哆嗦，
無奈那淒慘的雙腳，
乏得再不能前挪。

他雙臂將她抱緊，
一步一聲悲嘆，
一隻獅子忽現，
正臥在他們路前。

回轉去已是徒勞：
他用厚厚的鬃毛，

Bore them to the ground;
Then he stalk'd around,

Smelling to his prey.
But their fears allay,
When he licks their hands;
And silent by them stands.

They look upon his eyes
Fill'd with deep surprise:
And wondering behold,
A spirit arm'd in gold.

On his head a crown
On his shoulders down,
Flow'd his golden hair.
Gone was all their care.

'Follow me,' he said,
'Weep not for the maid;
In my palace deep,
Lyca lies asleep.'

Then they followed,
Where the vision led:
And saw their sleeping child,

把他們掀倒在地，
又大步繞來繞去，

他嗅著他的獵物。
他們卻稍稍膽壯，
他舔著他們的手，
靜靜地站在了一旁。

他們看他的眼睛，
感到無比地震驚：
他們驚奇地見到
一個金色的精靈。

他頭上戴著王冠，
毛髮從肩上披下，
他的毛髮如金，
他們的憂慮消盡。

「跟我來吧，」他說道：
「別再為姑娘哭了，
在我的深宮裡面
麗卡已安然入眠。」

那尤物前面走著，
他們在後面跟著：
他們見到孩子，

Among tygers wild.

To this day they dwell
In a lonely dell
Nor fear the wolfish howl,
Nor the lions' growl.

The Chimney Sweeper

A little black thing among the snow:
Crying 'weep, 'weep, in notes of woe!
'Where are thy father & mother? say?'
'They are both gone up to the church to pray.

'Because I was happy upon the heath,
And smil'd among the winter's snow:
They clothed me in the clothes of death,
And taught me to sing the notes of woe.

'And becuse I am happy & dance & sing,
They think they have done me no injury:
And are gone to praise God & his Priest & King
Who make up a heaven of our misery.'

在猛虎中間躺著。

他們直到今天,
都住在孤寂的山谷,
既不怕狼的嚎叫,
更不懼獅子的咆哮。

掃煙囪的孩子

雪地裡一個小黑點;
哭著掃,掃,叫人憐!
「你的爹娘在哪兒,說呀?」
「他們都去禮拜堂祈禱啦。」

「我在荒野裡曾經很快樂,
還在冬天的雪裡歡笑,
他們就讓我穿上黑衣,
叫我唱起悲傷的小調。

「我還是快樂,又跳又唱,
爹娘就以為沒把我害夠:
就去讚美上帝、神父和國王——
是他們在我們的苦難上建起天堂。」

Nurse's Song

When the voices of children are heard on the green
And whisprings are in the dale:
The days of my youth rise fresh in my mind,
My face turns green and pale.

'Then come home my children, the sun is gone down
And the dews of night arise
Your spring & your day, are wasted in play
And your winter and night in disguise.'

The Sick Rose

O Rose thou art sick!
The invisible worm
That flies in the night,
In the howling storm:

Has found out thy bed
Of crimson joy:
And his dark secret love
Does thy life destroy.

保母之歌

當孩子們的聲音從草坪傳來
耳語陣陣輕飄在山谷:
我的春光就生動地浮現在腦海:
我的臉發青,一會兒又泛白。

「該回來了,我的孩子,太陽落山了
夜間的露水也已經出來,
你們的春光和白晝在遊戲中荒廢了,
你們的白晝和夜晚在藉口中浪費了。」

枯萎的玫瑰

玫瑰啊,你枯萎了!
飛行在黑夜裡的
那無形的飛蟲
在嘯叫的風暴中:

找到了你的
緋紅色喜悅的床:
他的隱秘的愛情
毀了你的生命。

The Fly

Little Fly,
Thy summer's play
My thoughtless hand
Has brush'd away.

Am not I
A fly like thee?
Or art not thou
A man like me?

For I dance
And drink & sing;
Till some blind hand
Shall brush my wing.

If thought is life
And strength & breath:
And the want
Of thought is death;

Then am I
A happy fly,

蠅

小小的蠅兒,
你夏日的遊戲
已被我的手
不慎拂去了。

難道我不是
你一樣的蠅嗎?
你不也是
我一樣的人嗎?

我喝酒跳舞,
唱唱歌曲,
直到盲目的手
擦傷我翅翼。

若思想是生命
力量和呼吸,
而思想貧乏
就等於死去;

那我就是隻
幸福的蠅,

If I live,
Or if I die.

The Angel

I Dreamt a Dream! what can it mean?
And that I was a maiden Queen:
Guarded by an Angel mild;
Witless woe, was ne'er beguil'd!

And I wept both night and day
And he wip'd my tears away
And I wept both day and night
And hid from him my heart's delight.

So he took his wings and fled:
Then the morn blush'd rosy red:
I dried my tears & arm'd my fears
With ten thousand shields and spears.

Soon my Angel came again:
I was arm'd, he came in vain:
For the time of youth was fled
And grey hairs were on my head.

不管我活著，
還是死了。

天使

我做了個夢！它什麼意思？
在夢中我是個未婚女王，
由一個溫柔的天使守護；
愚蠢的悲哀，怎麼也止不住！

我日日夜夜不停地哭泣
並且天使他替我擦去淚滴，
日日夜夜我不停地哭泣
並且躲開他我才心中歡喜。

天使他拍起翅膀消失了；
黎明呈現出了玫瑰紅；
我擦乾眼淚，用十萬盾矛
來壓住我的惶惑驚恐。

不久，我的天使又來了；
我戒備著，他白來一趟：
我的青春已經消逝，
頭上已是白髮蒼蒼。

The Tiger

Tiger! Tiger! burning bright,
In the Forests of the Night:
What immortal hand or eye,
Could frame thy fearful symmetry?

In what distant deeps or skies
Burnt the fire of thine eyes?
On what wings dare he aspire?
What the hand dare sieze the fire?

And what shoulder, & what art,
Could twist the sinews of thy heart?
And when thy heart began to beat,
What dread hand? & what dread feet?

What the hammer? what the chain?
In what furnace was thy brain?
What the anvil? what dread grasp,
Dare its deadly terrors clasp?

When the stars threw down their spears
And water'd heaven with their tears:

虎

虎！虎！光焰灼灼，
燃燒在黑夜之林；
怎樣的神手和神眼
構造你可畏的美健？

在海與天多深的地方
燃著造你眼睛的火？
憑什麼翅膀他敢追它？
憑什麼手他敢捕捉？

憑什麼肩膀，什麼技藝，
才能擰成你的心肌？
何等可怖的手與腳才能
讓你的心臟開始搏擊？

用什麼錘子，什麼鐵鏈？
在什麼爐中將你的腦冶煉？
用什麼砧子？何等鐵手，
敢抓令凡人致命的物件？

當天上的群星投下長矛，
且用淚水浸濕了天空：

Did he smile his work to see?
Did he who made the Lamb make thee?

Tiger! Tiger! burning bright,
In the Forests of the Night:
What immortal hand or eye,
Dare frame thy fearful symmetry?

My Pretty Rose Tree

A flower was offerd to me;
Such a flower as May never bore.
But I said, 'I've a Pretty Rose-tree.'
And I passed the sweet flower o'er.

Then I went to my Pretty Rose-tree
To tend her by day and by night.
But my Rose turnd away with jealousy:
And her thorns were my only delight.

Ah! Sun-Flower

Ah Sun-flower! weary of time,
Who countest the steps of the Sun:

他在看著他的成果微笑？
是造耶穌的他將你創造？

虎！虎！光焰灼灼，
燃燒在黑夜之林；
怎樣的神手和神眼
構成你可畏的美健？

我美麗的玫瑰樹

有人獻給我一朵花兒，
一朵五月裡見不到的花兒；
但我說：「我有棵美麗的玫瑰樹。」
我放棄了那朵可愛的花兒。

我走向我的美麗的玫瑰樹，
日日夜夜我將她照顧，
但是她疑忌地轉過臉去，
她的刺成了我唯一的樂處。

太陽花

太陽花啊！厭倦了時間，
竟然數點起太陽的腳步，

Seeking after that sweet golden clime
Where the traveller's journey is done.

Where the Youth pined away with desire,
And the pale Virgin shrouded in snow:
Arise from their graves and aspire,
Where my Sun-flower wishes to go.

The Lilly

The modest Rose puts forth a thorn:
The humble Sheep, a threatning horn:
While the Lilly white, shall in Love delight,
Nor a thorn nor a threat stain her beauty bright.

The Garden of Love

I went to the Garden of Love,
And saw what I never had seen:
A Chapel was built in the midst,
Where I used to play on the green.

And the gates of this Chapel were shut,
And Thou shalt not writ over the door;

尋找那美妙的金色所在，
漫遊者結束旅程之處。

那裡，因情慾而憔悴的青年，
和裹著冰雪的蒼白的處女，
卻都從墳墓中起來，向往
我的太陽花想去的地方。

百合

羞怯的玫瑰豎著她的刺；
溫順的綿羊叉著嚇人的角；
而潔白的百合會用怡人的愛，
不用刺也不用角，來點染她輝煌的美。

愛的花園

我來到愛的花園裡面，
看到我從未見過的情形：
一座小教堂建在中央，
那兒原是我遊戲的草坪。

這座小教堂大門緊閉，
門上寫著「不准」的字樣；

So I turn'd to the Garden of Love,
That so many sweet flowers bore,

And I saw it was filled with graves,
And tomb-stones where flowers should be:
And Priests in black gowns, were walking their rounds,
And binding with briars, my joys & desires.

The Little Vagabond

Dear Mother, dear Mother, the Church is cold.
But the Ale-house is healthy & pleasant & warm;
Besides I can tell where I am use'd well.
Such usage in heaven will never do well.

But if at the Church they would give us some Ale,
And a pleasant fire, our souls to regale:
We'd sing and we'd pray, all the live-long day,
Nor ever once wish from the Church to stray;

Then the Parson might preach & drink & sing.
And we'd be as happy as birds in the spring:
And modest dame Lurch, who is always at Church,
Would not have bandy children nor fasting nor birch.

我於是轉向愛的花園，
許多花曾在那兒吐送芬芳；

現在我看到的卻是墳丘，
墓碑取代了昔日的花朵：
穿黑袍的神父來回轉悠，
用刺薔薇綑我的情慾和歡樂。

小流浪者

好媽媽，好媽媽，教堂裡真冷，
酒吧裡卻愜意暖和又益身；
我習慣待著的還有別的地方，
那樣的受用天堂裡也比不上。

但若在禮拜堂能給我們點啤酒，
給一盆好火烤起我們的精神；
我們願長長一整天地禱告歌唱，
一次也不想跑出去漂泊流浪。

牧師就可以講道、喝酒和唱歌，
我們會像春天的小鳥一樣快樂；
莊重的暗監夫人——她常在教堂，
就不會讓羅圈腿的孩子挨打挨餓。

And God like a father rejoicing to see
His children as pleasant and happy as he:
Would have no more quarrel with the Devil or the Barrel,
But kiss him & give him both drink and apparel.

London

I wander thro' each charter'd street,
Near where the charter'd Thames does flow.
And mark in every face I meet
Marks of weakness, marks of woe.

In every cry of every Man,
In every Infant's cry of fear,
In every voice, in every ban,
The mind-forg'd manacles I hear:

How the Chimney-sweeper's cry
Every black'ning Church appalls,
And the hapless Soldier's sigh,
Runs in blood down Palace walls.

But most thro' midnight streets I hear
How the youthful Harlot's curse
Blasts the new-born Infant's tear

上帝會像位父親高興,
看到孩子們跟自己同樣地幸福:
再也不會跟那個魔王或酒桶爭吵,
而是親吻他,給他酒又給他衣服。

倫敦

我走過每一條特轄大街,
附近特轄的泰晤士河的流淌。
我遇到的每一張臉上的痕跡
都表露出虛弱,表露出哀傷。

在每個人的每一聲呼叫之中,
在每個嬰兒害怕的哭聲裡,
在一聲一響,道道禁令中,
我聽到精神之枷鎖的碰擊:

掃煙囪的孩子的哭叫多麼
使每一個陰森的教堂懼怕,
還有那不幸的士兵的嘆息,
化成了鮮血從宮牆上淌下。

更不堪的是在夜半大街上
年輕妓女瘟疫般的詛咒,
吞噬了新生嬰兒的哭聲,

And blights with plagues the Marriage hearse.

The Human Abstract

Pity would be no more,
If we did not make somebody Poor:
And Mercy no more could be,
If all were as happy as we;

And mutual fear brings peace;
Till the selfish loves increase.
Then Cruelty knits a snare,
And spreads his baits with care.

He sits down with holy fears,
And waters the ground with tears:
Then Humility takes its root
Underneath his foot.

Soon spreads the dismal shade
Of Mystery over his head;
And the Catterpiller and Fly,
Feed on the Mystery.

把結婚喜榻變成了靈柩。

人之抽象

再也不會存在仁慈
若大家像我們一樣幸福,
同樣也不會有憐憫存在,
如果不使有的人窮苦;

彼此間的恐懼產生和睦,
一直到自私的愛增長。
於是殘忍就編織羅網,
細心地將誘餌播撒散布。

他懷著無比的敬畏坐下,
用他的淚水澆灌大地:
於是謙卑就在他腳下
伸出了它虯結的根鬚。

不久,他的頭頂上方
便佈下了神秘的暗影,
而對於那些毛蟲和蒼蠅,
神秘正是他們的食糧。

And it bears the fruit of Deceit,
Ruddy and sweet to eat;
And the Raven his nest has made
In its thickest shade.

The Gods of the earth and sea
Sought thro' Nature to find this Tree,
But their search was all in vain:
There grows one in the Human Brain.

Infant Sorrow

My mother groand! my father wept.
Into the dangerous world I leapt:
Helpless, naked, piping loud:
Like a fiend hid in a cloud.

Struggling in my father's hands:
Striving against my swaddling bands:
Bound and weary I thought best
To sulk upon my mother's breast.

它❷終於結出欺詐之果，
紅艷香甜，無比可口，
渡鴉❸用那濃濃的樹蔭
將他的巢穴造就。

陸上和海裡諸多神明
尋遍自然尋找此樹，
但他們只是枉尋一場；
人腦之中長著一株。

嬰兒的悲傷

我媽媽呻吟！我爸爸哭泣，
我跳進了這個危險世界裡；
赤條條無力自助，嘶嚎著：
像魔鬼藏在一片陰影裡。

在我爸爸手中掙扎著，
和我的襁褓拚命反抗著：
又被裹著，又累，我只想
在我媽媽的乳房上解氣。

---

❷指「謙卑」。

❸可能指神父。

A Poison Tree

I was angry with my friend:
I told my wrath, my wrath did end.
I was angry with my foe:
I told it not, my wrath did grow.

And I waterd it in fears,
Night & morning with my tears:
And I sunned it with smiles,
And with soft deceitful wiles.

And it grew both day and night.
Till it bore an apple bright.
And my foe beheld it shine,
And he knew that it was mine.

And into my garden stole.
When the night had veil'd the pole;
In the morning glad I see
My foe outstretch'd beneath the tree.

有毒的樹

我對朋友憤怒：
我表明憤怒，怒氣就沒了；
我對敵人憤怒：
我不予表露，這怒氣長著。

我提心吊膽將它澆灌，
日夜澆灌著淚滴；
我用微笑來將它照耀，
用軟軟的狡詐的詭計。

它日日夜夜地生長，
終於結出了鮮亮的蘋果。
我的敵人看到它閃光，
他知道那蘋果屬於我。

當夜色將樹身遮掩，
他就溜進園子裡偷食；
早晨我高興地看到
我的敵人在樹下挺屍。

A Little Boy Lost

'Nought loves another as itself
Nor venerates another so.
Nor is it possible to Thought
A greater than itself to know:

'And Father, how can I love you,
Or any of my brothers more?
I love you like the little bird
That picks up crumbs around the door.'

The Priest sat by and heard the child.
In trembling zeal he siez'd his hair:
He led him by his little coat:
And all admir'd the Priestly care.

And standing on the altar high,
'Lo what a fiend is here!' said he:
'One who sets reason up for judge
Of our most holy Mystery.'

少年之失

沒有人愛別人像愛自己，
也談不上那樣尊重別人，
比思想本身知道得更多，
對思想來說也不可能：

「父親❹啊，我怎能更加愛你，
或者更愛我的兄弟？
我愛你就像小小的鳥雀，
在門前啄食麵包的碎屑。」

神父坐在他旁邊諦聽，
激動地抓住他的頭髮：
他拽著小外衣揪牢這孩子：
大家都佩服這神父的心機。

他站在高高的祭壇之上：
「瞧，這兒有個惡魔！」
他說，「他竟捏造出論據
來指責我們最神聖的神秘。」

---

❹指上帝。

The weeping child could not be heard.
The weeping parents wept in vain:
They stripp'd him to his little shirt,
And bound him in an iron chain.

And burn'd him in a holy place,
Where many had been burn'd before:
The weeping parents wept in vain.
Are such things done on Albions shore?

A Little Girl Lost

Children of the future Age,
Reading this indignant page:
Know that in a former time,
Love! sweet Love! was thought a crime.

In the Age of Gold,
Free from winter's cold:
Youth and maiden bright,
To the holy light,
Naked in the sunny beams delight.

聽不見哭著的孩子的聲音，
哭著的雙親枉然地哭泣：
他被剝得只剩件小襯衣，
被用一根鐵鏈子捆起。

在一處聖地他被焚燒，
從前那兒焚燒過多人，
哭著的雙親枉然地哭泣，
這種事阿爾比恩❺海岸有嗎？

少女之失

未來時代的孩子們，
讀著這憤慨的一頁：
會知道從前的時候，
愛！甜蜜的愛！被當作罪孽。

在那黃金時代，
沒有冬天的寒冷：
歡快的青年男女，
於神聖的燈❻下，
在和煦的光中裸著遊戲。

---

❺英格蘭的古稱。

❻指太陽。

Once a youthful pair
Fill'd with softest care:
Met in garden bright,
Where the holy light,
Had just removed the curtains of the night.

There in rising day,
On the grass they play:
Parents were afar:
Strangers came not near:
And the maiden soon forgot her fear.

Tired with kisses sweet
They agree to meet,
When the silent sleep
Waves o'er heavens deep:
And the weary tired wanderers weep.

To her father white
Came the maiden bright:
But his loving look,
Like the holy book,
All her tender limbs with terror shook.

'Ona! pale and weak!
To thy father speak:

曾有對青年男女，
充滿了柔情蜜意：
相會在明亮的花園，
當神聖的燈，
剛剛拉去那夜的幕帘。

升起的曙光之中，
他們在草地上遊戲：
父母們不在近前，
陌生人遠離此地，
不久姑娘就忘記了恐懼。

親夠了甜蜜的吻，
他們約定要重逢，
在那安謐的睡夢
飄拂過深空：
而疲憊的旅人悲嘆的時辰。

善意的父親跟前，
來了歡快的少女：
但他那疼愛的神色，
就像那聖經，
她害怕得嬌軀抖抖瑟瑟。

「歐娜！你臉色蒼白！
快對你父親坦白：

O the trembling fear!
O the dismal care!
That shakes the blossoms of my hoary hair.'

To Tirzah

Whate'er is Born of Mortal Birth,
Must be consumed with the Earth
To rise from Generation free;
Then what have I to do with thee?

The Sexes sprung from Shame & Pride
Blow'd in the morn: in evening died.
But Mercy changd Death into Sleep;
The Sexes rose to work & weep.

Thou Mother of my Mortal part
With cruelty didst mould my Heart,
And with false self-decieving tears,
Didst bind my Nostrils, Eyes & Ears.

Didst close my Tongue in senseless clay,
And me to Mortal Life betray:

真讓人心兒發抖！
哦，憂愁啊！
真要把我的灰髮愁白。」

致特拉❼

出身於凡胎的芸芸眾生，
都將毀滅，消失軀體。
擺脫生殖而自由地復活：
那我何必和你在一起？

男女們出生於羞恥和驕傲，
在早晨開花，在黃昏死去。
但仁慈使死亡變成了安眠，
男女們復活了，激動哭泣。

你，我的凡體的母親，
用殘忍套住了我的心靈，
用那欺人又自欺的眼淚，
裹住我的鼻耳和眼睛。

用無知的泥土堵住我嘴，
使我背叛了塵世的生命：

---

❼不詳。可能是下文「我的凡體的母親」。

The Death of Jesus set me free;
Then what have I to do with thee?

The Schoolboy

I love to rise in a summer morn,
When the birds sing on every tree;
The distant huntsman winds his horn,
And the sky-lark sings with me.
O! what sweet company.

But to go to school in a summer morn,
O! it drives all joy away:
Under a cruel eye outworn,
The little ones spend the day,
In sighing and dismay.

Ah! then at times I drooping sit,
And spend many an anxious hour.
Nor in my book can I take delight,
Nor sit in learning's bower,
Worn thro' with the dreary shower.

耶穌之死使我無羈,
那我何必和你在一起?

小學生

我愛在夏天的清晨起床,
當鳥兒鳴囀在棵棵樹上;
獵人遠遠地吹著號角,
雲雀兒伴我歌唱,
啊!多美妙的夥伴。

但要在夏天的清晨上學,
唉!這把興致都掃盡:
在嚴厲昏花的眼底,
小同學們垂頭喪氣地
把一天苦熬過去。

唉!我有時得頹喪地坐著,
度過許多個急人的鐘點。
我得不到快樂,無論從書中,
或者看著板著的面孔,
在書齋裡面挫時間。

How can the bird that is born for joy,
Sit in a cage and sing?
How can a child when fears annoy,
But droop his tender wing,
And forget his youthful spring?

O! father & mother, if buds are nipp'd,
And blossoms blown away,
And if the tender plants are stripp'd
Of their joy in the springing day,
By sorrow and care's dismay,

How shall the summer arise in joy?
Or the summer fruits appear?
Or how shall we gather what griefs destroy?
Or bless the mellowing year,
When the blasts of winter appear?

The Voice of the Ancient Bard

Youth of delight come hither,
And see the opening morn:
Image of truth new born.
Doubt is fled & clouds of reason,
Dark disputes & artful teasing.

為了歡樂而出世的鳥兒
怎能坐在籠中歌唱？
孩子怎能一受驚擾就
垂下他嬌嫩的翅膀，
忘記了朝氣蓬勃的春天？

爸爸媽媽啊，若花蕾被摘，
花兒經不住風吹雨打去，
要是嫩弱的幼苗被悲哀
和滿腹的重重心事奪去
他們春天裡的歡愉，

夏天怎麼會高興地露頭，
夏天的果實怎麼會露臉？
怎收拾悲傷所毀的一切，
如何祝福豐美的一年，
當冬天的狂風出現？

古代吟遊詩人之聲

到這裡來吧，快樂的年輕人，
看這展布著的黎明：
這真理新生的象徵。
疑惑消失了，及理性的陰影，
及無知的爭辯和狡猾的戲弄。

Folly is an endless maze.
Tangled roots perplex her ways,
How many have fallen there!
They stumble all night over bones of the dead,
And feel they know not what but care:
And wish to lead others when they should be led.

A Divine Image

Cruelty has a Human Heart
And Jealousy a Human Face,
Terror, the Human Form Divine,
And Secrecy, the Human Dress.

The Human Dress, is forged Iron
The Human Form, a fiery Forge.
The Human Face, a Furnace seal'd,
The Human Heart, its hungry Gorge.

愚蠢是一條無盡的迷途，
糾結的根蔓困著她的路，
多少人在那裡被絆倒！
他們整夜在屍骨上跌躓，
還覺得想知道的他們全知道：
他們還需要引導，卻好為人師。

至上的形象

殘忍據有人的心靈，
嫉妒據有人的臉龐；
恐怖據有至上的人形，
隱秘據有人的服裝。

人的服裝是鍛過的鐵器，
人的外形是熊熊的鍛爐，
人的臉龐是封閉的熔爐，
人心是它的飢餓的胃部。

1789-1791

The Book of Thel

塞爾書

William Blake, *For Children: The Gates of Paradise*, object 5, 1793

Thel's Motto

Does the eagle know what is in the pit
Or wilt thou go ask the mole?
Can wisdom be put in a silver rod,
Or love in a golden bowl?

I
The daughters of Mne Seraphim led round their sunny flocks,
All but the youngest. She in paleness sought the secret air,
To fade away like morning beauty from her mortal day.
Down by the river of Adona her soft voice is heard,
And thus her gentle lamentation falls like morning dew:

'O life of this our spring, why fades the lotus of the water?
Why fade these children of the spring, born but to smile and fall?
Ah, Thel is like a watry bow, and like a parting cloud,
Like a reflection in a glass, like shadows in the water,
Like dreams of infants, like a smile upon an infant's face,
Like the dove's voice, like transient day, like music in the air;

塞爾的警句

難道鷹知道地洞裡有什麼？
否則你須去問鼴鼠，
難道智慧能存於銀箸之中？
愛能在金碗中存儲？

I
慕‧撒拉弗❶們的女兒一群群歡快地跳起圓舞，
唯有幼女不在：她神情黯淡地去尋找那片神秘的天去了，
像黎明美人一般從她的凡間的日子凋謝；
溫柔的聲音沿著阿多納河傳來，
她輕輕慟哭的聲音像晨露一樣降落：

「我們這一春的生命啊！水中的荷花為何凋謝？
為何凋謝了這些春天的孩子?她們只為了微笑和謝世而生。
啊！塞爾就像淡淡的彩虹，就像飄散的彩雲，
就像玻璃的反光，就像水中的倒影，
就像嬰兒的夢，像嬰兒臉上的一個微笑，
像鴿子的叫聲，像短暫的黎明，像空中的樂音。

---

❶布雷克對維納斯之使──六翼天使撒拉弗們的兒子們──的稱呼。

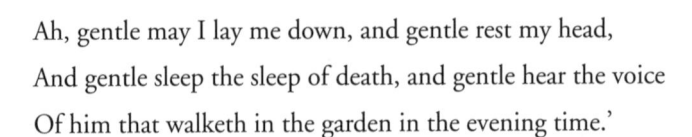

Ah, gentle may I lay me down, and gentle rest my head,
And gentle sleep the sleep of death, and gentle hear the voice
Of him that walketh in the garden in the evening time.'

The lily of the valley breathing in the humble grass
Answered the lovely maid, and said: 'I am a watry weed,
And I am very small, and love to dwell in lowly vales;
So weak, the gilded butterfly scarce perches on my head;
Yet I am visited from heaven, and he that smiles on all
Walks in the valley and each morn over me spreads his hand,
Saying, "Rejoice, thou humble grass, thou new-born lily flower,
Thou gentle maid of silent valleys and of modest brooks;
For thou shalt be clothed in light and fed with morning manna,
Till summer's heat melts thee beside the fountains and the springs
To flourish in eternal vales." Then why should Thel complain,
Why should the mistress of the vales of Har utter a sigh?'

She ceased and smiled in tears, then sat down in her silver shrine.
Thel answered: 'O thou little virgin of the peaceful valley,
Giving to those that cannot crave, the voiceless, the o'ertired.
Thy breath doth nourish the innocent lamb; he smells thy milky
   garments,

唉！我願輕輕躺下，輕輕地安放我的頭顱，
輕輕地進入長眠，平心靜氣地傾聽
黃昏時分他❷在花園中散步的聲音。」

溪谷中的百合在卑微的草叢中呼吸著，
她回應了可愛的少女並且說道：「我是棵水汪汪的野草。
我微不足道，愛住在淺淺的溪谷。
我太柔弱了，連金色蝴蝶也難以在我頭上駐足；
可是天上的來客訪問了我，對一切都微笑的他❸
在溪谷中散步，每天清晨都在我上空舖開手掌，
說道：「歡欣吧，你卑微的小草，你初開的百合花，
你寂靜的溪谷中和素樸的小徑上溫柔的少女
歡欣吧，因為你將沐著光明，飲著黎明的嗎哪❹，
直到夏天的暑熱在噴泉和流水旁將你融化，
使你在永恒的谷中繁茂。那塞爾你為何還要抱怨？
為何哈爾溪谷的女主人還要發出嘆息之聲？」

她說完了，含淚微笑著，在她的銀色神龕中坐下。

塞爾答道：「你平靜的溪谷中的小小處女啊，
歸於那些不會請求的，沉默的、精疲力竭的眾生。
你的呼吸哺育著天真的羊羔，他嗅著你含乳的外衣。

---

❷❸上帝。

❹一種神賜的食物。《聖經》記載以色列人出埃及時，靠它生
　活了二十年。

He crops they flowers, while thou sittest smiling in his face,
Wiping his mild and meekin mouth from all contagious taints.
Thy wine doth purify the golden honey; thy perfume,
Which thou dost scatter on every little blade of grass that springs,
Revives the milked cow and tames the fire-breathing steed.
But Thel is like a faint cloud kindled at the rising sun:
I vanish from my pearly throne, and who shall find my place?'

'Queen of the vales', the lily answered, 'ask the tender cloud,
And it shall tell thee why it glitters in the morning sky,
And why it scatters its bright beauty through the humid air.
Descend, O little cloud, and hover before the eyes of Thel.'

The cloud descended, and the lily bowed her modest head,
And went to mind her numerous charge among the verdant grass.

II
'O little cloud', the virgin said, 'I charge thee, tell to me
Why thou complainest not, when in one hour thou fade away.
Then we shall seek thee but not find; ah, Thel is like to thee,
I pass away; yet I complain, and no one hears my voice.'

The cloud then showed his golden head, and his bright form emerged,
Hovering and glittering on the air before the face of Thel:

'O virgin, knowest thou not? Our steeds drink of the golden springs

他嚙著你的花兒,而你卻坐著,對他微笑,
擦去他的嫩齒上所有會感染的污跡,
你的酒潔淨了金色的蜜;你的芬芳
灑在每一棵小草所綻開的葉片上
使乳牛重新產奶,將火烈的駿馬馴服,
可是,塞爾卻像一片被旭日照亮的薄雲:
我從我的珍珠寶座上消隱了,誰會發現我的去處?」

「溪谷的女王」,百合答道:「問柔雲去吧,
它將告訴你,它為何在晨空中熠熠生輝,
它為何在濕潤的天上遍灑輝煌的美。
下來吧,小小的雲兒,在塞爾眼前盤旋。」

雲下來了,於是百合點了點她端莊的頭,
到綠草叢中照顧她眾多的托管者去了。

II
「小小的雲啊,」那處女說道:「我要你告訴我
你為何無憂無怨,儘管你一個鐘頭就會消散,
然後我們將找尋你,卻無從尋覓:唉!塞爾像你一樣:
我消逝了:然而我抱怨,又沒有誰聽到我的聲音。」

雲於是炫耀著金色的頭,顯現出輝煌的形象,
在塞爾面前的空中閃爍和盤旋:

「處女啊,你可知道,我們的駿馬飲著金色泉水,

Where Luvah doth renew his horses. Lookest thou on my youth,
And fearest thou because I vanish and am seen no more,
Nothing remains? O maid, I tell thee, when I pass away
It is to tenfold life, to love, to peace, and raptures holy.
Unseen descending weigh my light wings upon balmy flowers,
And court the fair-eyed dew to take me to her shining tent.
The seeping virgin trembling kneels before the risen sun,
Till we arise linked in a golden band and never part,
But walk united, bearing food to all our tender flowers.'

'Dost thou, O little cloud? I fear that I am not like thee;
For I walk through the vales of Har, and smell the sweetest flowers,
But I feed not the little flowers; I hear the warbling birds,
But I feed not the warbling birds. They fly and seek their food.
But Thel delights in these no more, because I fade away;
And all shall say, "without a use this shining woman lived —
Or did she only live to be at death the food of worms?"'
The cloud reclined upon his airy throne and answered thus:
'Then if thou art the food of worms, O virgin of the skies,
How great thy use, how great thy blessing! Every- thing that lives
Lives not alone, nor for itself. Fear not and I will call
The weak worm from its lowly bed, and thou shalt hear its voice.

泉邊，魯法❺使他的駿馬得到了復原？展望我的青春，
你感到害怕，是因為我煙消霧散不復出現，
一無所留？姑娘啊，我告訴你，我消逝
是去得到十倍的生命，得到愛、平靜和神聖的狂喜：
我將無形地下降，在芬芳的鮮花上壓上我輕盈的翅膀，
向碧眼的露珠求愛，住進她閃閃發光的寓所：
那哭泣的處女，將顫抖著，跪在升起的太陽之前，
直到我們用金帶連在一起上升，一起散步，
永不分離，為我們所有嬌嫩的花提供食物。」

「是嗎，啊，小小的雲？恐怕我不像你，
當我漫步穿過哈爾溪谷，我聞著鮮花的芬芳，
卻不餵養小小花兒；我聽著鳥兒的鳴囀，
卻不餵養鳴囀的鳥兒：牠們飛行並自己尋找食物：
但塞爾不再因此而快樂，因為我消逝了；
而且大家會說：「這出眾的女子活著毫無用處，
或許她活著是為了死時充當蚯蚓的食物。」

雲斜倚在他空中的寶座上，這樣答道：

「即使你是蚯蚓的食物，天上的處女啊，
你也有多大的用處，多麼好的運氣！世間眾生
不是獨自也不是為己而活著：別害怕，我要為你
叫來地床中柔弱的蚯蚓，你會聽到牠的聲音。

---

❺ 布雷克的宗教神話體系中的神之一，代表感情。

Come forth, worm of the silent valley, to thy pensive queen.'

The helpless worm arose, and sat upon the lily's leaf,
And the bright cloud sailed on to find his partner in the vale.

III
Then Thel astonished viewed the worm upon its dewy bed:
'Art thou a worm, image of weakness? Art thou but a worm?
I see thee like an infant wrapped in the lily's leaf.
Ah, weep not; little voice, thou canst not speak, but thou canst weep.
Is this a worm? I see thee lay helpless and naked weeping,
And none to answer, none to cherish thee with mother's smiles.'

The clod of clay heard the worm's voice and raised her pitying head;
She bowed over the weeping infant and her life exhaled
In milky fondness; then on Thel she fixed her humble eyes:

'O beauty of the vales of Har, we live not for ourselves;
Thou seest me, the meanest thing, nad so I am indeed;
My bosom of itself is cold and of itself is dark,
But he that loves the lowly pours his oil upon my head,
And kisses me, and binds his nuptial bands around my breast,
And says; "Thou mother of my children, I have loved thee,
And I have given thee a crown that none can take away.'

出來吧,平靜的溪谷中的蚯蚓,見你憂鬱的女王。」

孤弱的蚯蚓出現了,坐在百合的葉子上,
輝煌的雲繼續航行,找他溪谷中的夥伴去了。

III
塞爾驚奇地看到了棲在沾著露珠的褥墊上的蚯蚓:
「你是一條蚯蚓?柔弱的形象,你只是一條蚯蚓?
我看到你好像裹在百合葉裡的嬰兒
啊,莫哭,小小的聲音;你不會講話,卻會哭泣。
難道這是條蚯蚓?我看你赤著裸躺著,哭著
沒有誰理睬,沒有誰用母親的微笑來愛撫你。」

土塊聽到了蚯蚓的哭聲,抬起了她憐愛的臉,
她向哭著的嬰兒俯下身子,她的生命裡
散發出溺愛的乳香;然後向塞爾投去謙卑的目光:

「哈爾溪谷的美人啊,我們不是為自己生活,
你看到了我,這最卑賤的東西,我確實很卑賤:
我的胸本來是冰涼的,本來是黑色的。
然而愛卑賤者的他❻,在我的頭上灑了他的油,
並吻了我,用他的結婚禮帶束了我的胸,
說:「你,我的孩子的母親,我愛上了你,
我給了你誰也奪不走的花冠。」

---

❻上帝。

But how this is, sweet maid, I know not, and I cannot know,
I ponder, and I cannot ponder; yet I live and love.'

The daughter of beauty wiped her pitying tears with her white veil
And said: 'Alas! I knew not this, and therefore did I weep.
That God would love a worm I knew, and punish the evil foot
That wilful bruised its helpless form. But that he cherished it
With milk and oil I never knew, and therefore did I weep,
And I complained in the mild air, because I fade away
And lay me down in thy cold bed and leave my shining lot.'

'Queen of the vales', the matron clay answered, 'I heard thy sighs.
And all thy moans flew o'er my roof but I have called them down.
Wilt thou, O Queen, enter my house—'tis given thee to enter
And to return. Fear nothing; enter with thy virgin feet.'

IV
The eternal gates' terrific porter lifted the northern bar.
Thel entered in and saw the secrets of the land unknown.
She saw the couches of the dead, and where the fibrous roots
Of every heart on earth infixes deep its restless twists:
A land of sorrows and of tears where never smile was seen.

She wandered in the land of clouds, through valleys dark, listening
Dolours and lamentations; waiting oft beside a dewy grave
She stood in silence, listening to the voices of the ground,

但這是怎麼回事,我不知也無法知道,可愛的姑娘;
我默默地想,又想不出什麼;然而我活著並且愛著。」

那美的女兒用潔白的面紗擦著同情的淚水,
說道:「哎!我不知道這一切,所以我哭了;
我知道上帝會愛一條蚯蚓、會懲罰
那故意傷害他孤弱的形象的腳,但我不知
他用乳汁和油來撫愛它,所以我哭了。
我在和暖的空中發出過怨言,因為我凋謝了、
在你冰冷的床上躺下、離開了我的光輝的命運。」

「溪谷的女王,」土塊主婦答:「我聽到了你的嘆息,
你所有的悲嘆飛過我的屋頂,但我把它們叫了下來。
你願意到我的屋裡去嗎,啊,女王?它給你進去,
也讓你出來:別怕,抬起你處女的纖足進去吧。」

IV
永恒之門可怕的看守者移開了向北的柵欄,
塞爾走進去,看到了未知國度的秘密。
她看到死者的臥榻,看到了每顆心堅韌的根,
都把它不知足的鬚鬚深深地嵌入土中:
那是永遠見不到微笑的、悲傷與眼淚的國度。

她在那不見天日的國度裡徘徊,穿過黑暗溪谷,聽見
憂傷的悲泣的聲音;她時常靜靜地守候
在覆著露水的墓地,聆聽土地中的聲響,

Till to her own grave plot she came, and there she sat down,
And heard this voice of sorrow breathed from the hollow pit:

'Why cannot the ear be closed to its own destruction?
Or the glistening eye to the posion of a smile?
Why are the eyelids stored with arrows ready drawn,
Where a thousand fighting men in ambush lie?
Or an eye of gifts and graces, showering fruits and coined gold?
Why a tongue impressed with honey from every wind?
Why an ear a whirlpool fierce to draw creations in?
Why a nostril wide inhaling terror, trembling and affright?
Why a tender curb upon the youthful burning boy?
Why a little curtain of flesh on the bed of our desire?'

The virgin started from her seat, and with a shriek
Fled back unhindered till she came into the vales of Har.

最後她來到自己的墓旁,席地而坐;
她聽到那空空的洞穴中傳來這樣的哀鳴:

「為何耳不能對自己的毀滅掩而不聞?
為何閃亮的眼不能對微笑之鴆毒閉而不視?
為何眼瞼中藏匿著待機而發的箭矢,
使成千上萬的戰鬥者喪生於暗中的伏擊?
為何一隻充滿天賦和魅力的眼展示出果實和金幣?
為何一條舌頭敷上了每一陣風送來的蜜?
為何一扇耳朵,一個凶猛的漩渦把創造物捲進去?
為何一翼闊大的鼻吸著戰慄的恐怖和驚懼?
為何一個脆弱的羈絆阻礙了熱血少年?
為何一幅小小的肉的幕簾罩在我們的慾望之床前?」

聽到這,那處女一聲尖叫,頭也不回,
慌不擇路地往回逃,遁入了哈爾溪谷。

1793

Visions of the Daughters of Albion
阿爾比恩女兒們的夢幻

William Blake, *For Children: The Gates of Paradise*, object 15, 1793

The Argument

I loved Theotormon,
And I was not ashamed;
I trembled in my virgin fears,
And I bid in Leutha's vale.

I plucked Leutha's vale.
I plucked Leutha's flower,
And I rose up from the vale;
But the terrible thunders tore
My virgin mantle in twain.

Visions

Enslaved, the daughters of Albion weep–a trembling lamentation
Upon their mountains, in their valleys sighs toward America.
For the soft soul of America, Oothoon, wandered in woe
Along the vales of Leutha, seeking flowers to comfort her;
And thus she spoke to the bright marigold of Leutha's vale:

'Art thou a flower? Art thou a nymph? I see thee now a flower,
  Now a nymph! I dare not pluck thee from thy dewy bed.'

梗概

我愛塞歐托曼,
心中一片坦然;
我含著處女的淚顫抖,
藏在柳薩的溪畔!

我採擷柳薩的花朵,
從溪谷向上登攀;
但是那可怕的雷霆
將我的處女罩撕作兩半。

夢幻

受著奴役,阿爾比恩的女兒們哭泣:從她們的山巒
慟哭聲震顫;從她們的溪谷為亞美利加發出嘆息。
奧松——亞美利加溫柔的靈魂,正沿著柳薩溪谷
悲傷地遊蕩,尋找花兒來安慰她自己。
她對柳薩溪谷的金瑪麗花說出這樣的話:

「你是花兒,還是美女?我看你剛才是花兒,
現在卻是美女!我不敢從你凝露的花床上摘下你!」

The golden nymph replied:' Pluck thou my flower, Oothoon the mild. Another flower shall spring, because the soul of sweet delight Can never pass away.' She ceased and closed her golden shrine.

Then Oothoon plucked the flower, saying, 'I pluck thee from thy bed, Sweet flower, and put thee here to glow between my breasts, And thus I turn my face to where my whole soul seeks.'

Over the waves she went in winged exulting swift delight,
And over Theotormon's reign took her impetuous course.

Bromion rent her with his thunders; on his stormy bed
Lay the faint maid, and soon her woes appalled his thunders hoarse.

Bromion spoke: 'Behold this harlot here on Bromion's bed,
And let the jealous dolphins sport around the lovely maid!
Thy soft American plains are mine, and mine thy north and south.
Stamped with my signet are the swarthy children of the sun;
They are obedient, they resist not, they obey the scourge;
Their daughters worship terrors and obey the violent.
Now thou maist marry Bromion's harlot and protect the child
Of Bromion's rage that Oothoon shall put forth in nine moons time.'

Then storms rent Theotormon's limbs; he rolled his waves around

金色的美女答:「摘去我的花吧,溫柔的奧松,
摘一朵還會長一朵,充滿甜蜜的喜悅的靈魂
永遠不會逝去。」她說完後便合上金色的神龕。

奧松摘下花兒,說道:「芬芳的鮮花啊,
我從你的床上摘下你,讓你在我胸間煥發榮光,
我要這樣帶著你,奔向整個靈魂想往的地方。」

她越過波浪,帶著有翼的、迅捷若狂的喜悅
在塞歐托曼的王國上空疾速飛馳。

然而布羅明的雷霆擄走了她;這柔弱的少女躺在
他的風暴之床上,她的悲傷不久便嚇壞了他的雷霆。

布羅明嘲弄塞歐托曼道:「看啊,看我床上這妓女,
讓嫉妒的海豚圍著這可愛的姑娘遊戲吧。
你柔軟的亞美利加平原屬於我,還有你的南方北方:
打上了我的印記的是太陽的黝黑的孩子們;
他們馴服,他們不固執,他們服從鞭子;
他們的女兒崇拜恐怖並且順從暴力。
現在你可以娶布羅明的妓女了,你得保護好
布羅明的狂怒之子,九個月後奧松會生下他。」

暴怒撕扯著塞歐托曼的四肢:他抓起滾滾波濤

And folded his black jealous waters round the adulterate pair.
Bound back to back in Bromion's caves, terror and meekness dwell.
At entrance Theotormon sits, wearing the threshold hard
With secret tears; beneath him sound like waves on a desert shore
The ovice of slaves beneath the sun, and children bought with money,
That shiver in religious caves beneath the burning fires
Of lust that belch incessant from the summits of the earth.

Oothoon weeps not, she cannot weep, her tears are locked up,
But she can howl incessant, writhing fer soft snowy limbs
And calling Theotormon's eagles to prey upon her flesh:

'I call with holy voice kings of the sounding air,
Rend away this defiled bosom that I may reflect
The image of Theotormon on my pure transparent breast.'

The eagles at her call descend and rend their bleeding prey.
Theotormon severely smiles; her soul reflects the smile,
As the clear spring muddied with feet of beasts grows pure & smiles.

The daughters of Albion hear her woes, and echo back her sighs.

'Why does my Theotormon sit weeping upon the threshold,
And Oothoon hovers by his side, persuading him in vain?
I cry, Arise, O Theotormon, for the village dog
Barks at the breaking day, the nightingale has done lamenting,

放出滔滔黑水,將那犯姦的一對團團圍住。
恐怖和溫順被背對背綁著,丟在布羅明的洞裡。
塞歐托曼坐在洞口悄然無聲地哭泣,淚水浸透了
堅硬的門檻;像波濤沖擊著海岸,他的下方響著
陽光下奴隸的聲音,金錢所買來的孩子們的聲音。
他們在修道之洞中,在熊熊的色慾之火中顫抖,
那火焰,從地球的絕頂,不斷向外噴射。

奧松不再哭,她已哭不出!她的淚泉已經乾涸,
但她還能不斷號叫,她扭動著雪白柔軟的身子,
呼喚塞歐托曼的鷹來啄食她肉體:

「我以聖潔的聲音呼喚你們,喧囂的天空之王啊,
請撕去這被玷污的胸膛,讓我能夠
在純潔透明的胸上,映照出塞歐托曼的形象。」

鷹聽從了她的呼喚,飛下來撕食血淋淋的食物。
塞歐托曼莊重地笑了:她的靈魂映出了這笑容,
宛如野獸踩髒的明淨春天重獲純潔,展露笑顏。

阿爾比恩的女兒們聽到她的不幸,回應了她的嘆息。

為何我的塞歐托曼坐在門檻上哭個不停,
奧松我在他身旁徘徊,勸慰他,白費唇舌?
我要吶喊:塞歐托曼,起來吧,在這破曉時分
狗在吠叫,夜鶯已經唱完她的悲歌,

The lark does rustle in the ripe corn, and the eagle returns
From nighty prey and lifts his golden beak to the pure east,
Shaking the dust from his immortal pinions to awake
The sun that sleeps too long. Arise, my Theotormon, I am pure!
Because the night is gone that closed me in its deadly black.
They told me that the night and day were all that I could see;
They told me that I had five senses to enclose me up,
And they enclosed my infinite brain into a narrow circle
And sunk my heart into the abyss, a red round globe hotburning,
Till all from life I was obliterated and erased.
Instead of morn arises a bright shadow, like an eye
In the eastern cloud, instead of night a sickly charnel-house,
That Theotormon hears me not. To him the night and morn
Are both alike–a night of sighs, a morning of fresh tears,
And none but Bromion can hear my lamentations.

'With what sense is it that the chicken shuns the ravenous hawk?
With what sense does the tame pigeon measure out the expanse?
With what sense does the bee form cells? Have not the mouse &
frog Eyes and ears and sense of touch? Yet are their habitations
And their pursuits as different as their forms and as their joys.
Ask the wild ass why he refuses burdens and the meek camel
Why he loves man. Is it because of eye, ear, mouth or skin,
Or breathing nostrils? No! for these the wolf and tiger have.
Ask the blind worm the secrets of the grave, and why her spires
Love to curl round the bones of death; and ask the ravenous snake

百靈在成熟的谷地裡覓食,鷹停止了夜間的捕獵
已經迴返,他給純潔的東方留下了金色的喙,
用非凡的翅膀扇起塵土,喚醒了睡得太久的
太陽。起來吧,我的塞歐托曼,我是純潔的,
那把我禁閉在死寂的黑暗中的夜,已經去了。
他們告訴我,我能看到的只有黑夜與白晝,
他們告訴我,我有把自己密閉起來的五官,
他們把我無限的大腦關進了一個狹小的圈子,
使我的心沉入深淵——一個灼灼燃燒的火球,
最後把我從生活中徹底抹去。
升起的不是太陽,而是一個亮影,像東方雲霞中
一隻眼睛;降臨的不是黃昏,而是陰沉的太平間啊,
塞歐托曼不聽我說。對於他,黎明和黃昏
都一樣——黃昏嘆息,黎明又流出新的淚水
除了布羅明,誰也聽不見我慟哭的聲音。

雞雛憑什麼感官來逃避貪婪的鷹隼?
鴿子憑什麼感官來測度浩瀚的太空?
蜜蜂憑什麼感官來營造蜂房?老鼠和青蛙
難道就沒有觸覺器官?只不過他們的習慣和追求
隨他們形狀和喜好的不同而不同。
問一問野驢他為何不肯載重,問一問溫順的駱駝
他為何熱愛人類:是因為有眼睛耳朵嘴巴皮膚
或因為有鼻子呼吸?不,這一些虎狼也有。
向沒有眼睛的蚯蚓問一問墳墓的秘密吧,問問她
為何將愛盤繞在屍骨上;問一問貪婪的蛇她的毒液

Where she gets poison, and the winged eagle why he loves the sun;
And then tell me the thoughts of man that have been hid of old.

'Silent I hover all the night, and all day could be silent,
If Theotormon once would turn his loved eyes upon me.
How can I be defiled when I reflect thy image pure?
Sweetest the fruit that the worm feeds on, and the soul preyed on by woe,
The new-washed lamb tinged with the village smoke, and the bright swan
By the red earth of our immortal river. I bathe my wings,
And I am white and pure to hover round Theotormon's breast.'

Then Theotormon broke his silence, and he answered:

'Tell me what is the night or day to one o'erflowed with woe?
Tell me what is a thought, and of what substance it is made?
Tell me what is a joy and in what gardens do joys grow.
And in what rivers swim the sorrows, and upon what mountains
Wave shadows of discontent, and in what houses dwell the wretched
Drunken with woe, forgotten and shut up from cold despair?

'Tell me where dwell the thoughts forgotten till thou call them forth,
Tell me where dwell the joys of old, and where the ancient loves.
And when will they renew again and the night of oblivion past,
That I might traverse times and spaces far remote, and bring

來自何方,問一問有翼的鷹他為何熱愛太陽,
然後告訴我昔日人們被掩藏起來的思想。

默默無言地我整夜徘徊,我能整日默默無言,
只要塞歐托曼你向我投一瞥含情的目光。
我純潔地映出了你的形象,怎能被玷污?
蛆蟲愛吃的果子最甜,悲傷啃嚙的靈魂最美,
被凡塵之河中的紅色泥土染上了炊煙氣息
和鮮艷的天鵝色的、新洗禮的羊羔
最最新鮮。我梳洗了翅膀,
繞著塞歐托曼的胸盤旋,我一身潔白。

於是塞歐托曼打破了自己的沉默,他答道:

告訴我,對於一個充滿悲傷的人,什麼是畫與夜?
告訴我什麼是思想,它由什麼物質造成?
告訴我什麼是歡樂,它在什麼花園中生長?
什麼河流中游著悲傷?什麼山上
搖曳著失意者的影像?什麼屋中住著不幸者,
飲著忘卻的悲哀,關門避開了冷酷的絕望?

告訴我哪裡住著忘卻的思念,在你沒有喚醒它們的時辰?
告訴我哪裡住著昔日的歡樂?哪裡住著過去的愛情?
它們何時再醒來,還有被遺忘了的那些逝去的夜晚?
告訴我,讓我可以久遠地橫越時空,把慰藉

Comforts into a present sorrow and a night of pain?
Where goest thou, O thought? To what remote land is thy flight?
If thou returnest to the present moment of affliction
Wilt thou bring comforts on thy wings, and dews and honey and balm,
Or poison from the desert wilds, from the eyes of the envier?'

Then Bromion said, and shook the cavern with his lamentation:

'Thou knowest that the ancient trees seen by thine eyes have fruit,
But knowest thou that trees and fruits flourish upon the earth
To gratify senses unknown, trees, beasts and birds unknown;
Unknown, not unperceived, spread in the infinite microscope,
In places yet unvisited by the voyager, and in worlds
Over another kind of seas, and in atmospheres unknown?
Ah, are there other wars beside the wars of sword and fire?
And are there other sorrows besides the sorrows of poverty?
And are there other joys beside the joys of riches and ease?
And is there not one law for both the lion and the ox?
And is there not eternal fire–and eternal chains
To bind the phantoms of existence from eternal life?'
Then Oothoon waited silent all the day and all the night,
But when the morn arose, her lamentation renewed.

The daughters of Albion hear heer woes, and echo back her sights.

帶進悲傷的現在和痛苦的黑夜。
思念啊，你哪裡去了，飛向了哪一片遙遠的土地？
如果你飛回到現在這苦惱的時刻，
你可會用翅膀載來慰藉、甘露、蜜和香脂，
要不載來毒素，從荒野裡、從嫉妒者眼中？」

布羅明的慟哭搖撼著洞穴。塞歐托曼接著說道：

你知道你親眼看見過的古樹結了果，
但你是否知道那樹在大地上繁衍是為了
滿足未知的感官——未知的樹木、動物和鳥兒？
它們未知，但並非未被察覺，它們在無限之顯微鏡中，
在尚未航行到的地方，在另一種海洋
上空的世界裡，在未知的大氣層中擴展著，
啊！除了劍與火的戰爭之外，可還有別的戰爭？
除了貧窮的苦惱之外，可還有別的苦惱？
除了富有和安逸的歡樂之外，可還有別的歡樂？
是否有一條既能束獅子又能約束牛的法律？
是否有永恆的火焰與永恆的鎖鏈
從永恆的生命中縛住存在之幽靈？
於是奧松整日整夜地默默等待著，
可是當黎明升起的時候，她又開始慟哭。

阿爾比恩的女兒們聽到她的不幸，回應了她的嘆息。

'O Urizen! creator of men, mistaken Demon of heaven
Thy joys are tears, thy labour vain, to form men to thine image.
How can one joy absorb another? Are not different joys
Holy, eternal, infinite? And each joy is a love.

'Does not the great mouth laugh at a gift, and the narrow eyelids mock
At the labour that is above payment? And wilt thou take the ape
For thy counsellor, or the dog for a schoolmaster to thy children?
Does he who contemns poverty, and he who turns with abhorrence
From usury, feel the same passion—or are they moved alike?
How can the giver of gifts experience the delights of the merchant,
How the industrious citizen the pains of the husbandman?
How different far the fat-fed hireling with hollow drum,
Who buys whole cornfields into wastes and sings upon the heath!
How different their eye and ear! How different the world to them!
With what sense does the parson claim the labour of the farmer?
What are his nets and gins and traps, and how does he surround him
With cold floods of abstraction and with forests of solitude,
To build him castles and high spires, where kings and priests may dwell,
Till she who burns with youth and knows no fixed lot, is bound
In spells of law to one she loathes. And must she drag the chain
Of life in weary lust? Must chilling murderous thoughts obscure
The clear heaven of her eternal spring, to bear the wintry rage
Of a harsh terror, driven to madness, bound to hold a rod
Over her shrinking shoulders all the day, and all the night

尤利壬❶啊！人的創造者！你錯了，天上的守護神！
你的歡樂成了眼淚，你徒然按你的形象辛辛苦苦造了人。
一種歡樂何必同化於另一種？難道不同的歡樂
不就是神聖、無窮和永恒？每一種歡樂都是一種愛。

你沒看見巨大的嘴在為禮物而笑？狹隘的眼瞼
在嘲笑超然於報酬的勞動？難道你會用猿
作你的顧問？請狗作你孩子的教師？
難道蔑視貧困者與厭惡高利貸者
會有同樣的激情，受類似的感動？
禮物的給予者怎能體驗到商人的快樂？
勤勞的市民怎能體驗到農民的痛苦？
他買下整片小麥地使之荒蕪，在荒野上歌唱：
兩種人眼與耳何等地不同，世界對於他們多麼地兩樣！
牧師索取農夫的勞動時心中是什麼感覺？
他用什麼作羅網、圈套和陷阱？他怎樣用抽象之冷水
圍著自己，怎樣用孤寂之林為自己建造國王和神父
享用的城堡和高聳的塔尖；最後用律法的符咒
將燃燒著青春之火而不懂得既定命運的她，綁在
她憎惡的人身上？難道她必須在令人厭倦的肉慾中
拖著生命的鎖鏈？難道令人心寒的凶殺之念，定要
遮蔽她永恒之春的明淨天空；為了承受令人發狂的
嚴酷而恐怖的冬日風暴，定要整天把棍棒
高懸在她蜷縮的身體上方，定要整夜地

---

❶布雷克宗教神話體系中的神之一，代表理性。

To turn the wheel of false desire, and longings that wake her womb
To the abhorred birth of cherubs in the human form,
That live a pestilence and die a meteor and are no more;
Till the child dwell with one he hates, and do the deed he loathes,
And the impure scourge force his seed into its unripe birth
Ere yet his eyelids can behold the arrows of the day?

'Does the whale worship at thy footsteps as the hungry dog,
Or does he scent the mountain prey, because his nostrils wide
Draw in the ocean? Does his eye discern the flying cloud
As the raven's eye, or does he measure the expanse like the vulture?
Does the still spider view the cliffs where eagles hide their young?
Or does the fly rejoice, because the harvest is brought in?
Does not the eagle scorn the earth and despise the treasures beneath?
But the mole knoweth what is there, and the worm shall tell it thee.
Does not the worm erect a pillar in the mouldering churchyard
And a palace of eternity in the jaws of the hungry grave?
Over his porch these words are written: 'Take thy bliss, O Man!
And sweet shall be thy taste, and sweet thy infant joys renew!'

'Infancy! fearless, lustful, happy, nestling for delight
In laps of pleasure: Innocence, honest, open, seeking
The vigorous joys of morning light, open to virgin bliss,
Who taught thee modesty, subtle modesty, child of night and sleep?
When thou awakest, wilt thou dissemble all thy secret joys,
Or wert thou not awake when all this mystery was disclos'd?

轉動虛假慾望之輪,轉動那喚醒她子官渴望的輪子,
使她終於生出那些人形的小天使——
這些孩子生如瘟疫,死若流星,歸於寂滅;
他們與自己所恨的人同居,違心地行事,
下流的鞭子造成他們的後代早產,
而他們的眼瞼最終看見了白晝之箭?

難道鯨崇拜你那餓狗一般的步履?
難道他嗅出巨大的獵物,是因為他的鼻子
在海洋中伸出去很遠?難道他的眼睛辨別飛雲
像渡鴉的眼睛一樣?或像禿鷲一樣測度浩翰?
難道靜臥的蜘蛛能看到藏著幼鷹的懸崖?
難道蒼蠅會為了人門取得豐收而歡欣?
難道鷹藐視大地,鄙視地下的寶藏?
只有鼴鼠知道地下有什麼,只有蚯蚓會告訴你。
難道蚯蚓不是在坍塌的教堂庭院裡豎起了柱子?
在飢餓的墳墓之顎上豎起了永恒的官殿?
它的入口上方寫著這些話:「人子啊,取走你的福,
你的體驗將是甜蜜的,你童稚的歡樂將甜蜜地甦醒!」

嬰兒期!它無畏、貪慾、幸福,為了歡樂
而在愉悅山坳中築巢:天真!它誠實、坦白,追求
晨光的朝氣蓬勃的歡樂,向純潔的狂喜敞開胸懷。
夜晚與睡眠的孩子,誰教會你羞怯:狡猾的羞怯?
你醒來時可會掩飾你所有秘密的歡樂,
難道你在這一切神秘被披露時沒有醒來?

Then com'st thou forth a modest virgin, knowing to dissemble,
With nets found under thy night pillow to catch virgin joy,
And brand it with the name of whore, and sell it in the night,
In silence, even without a whisper, and inseeming sleep.
Religious dreams and holy vespers light thy smoky fires:
Once were thy fires lighted by the eyes of honest morn.
And does my Theotormon seek this hypocrite modesty,
This knowing, artful, secret, fearful, cautious, trembling hypocrite?

Then is Oothoon a whore indeed! and all the virgin joys
Of life are harlots, and Theotormon is a sick man's dream;
And Oothoon is the crafty slave of selfish holiness.

But Oothoon is not so, a virgin filled with virgin fancies,
Open to joy and to delight wherever beauty appears.
If in the morning sun I find it, there my eyes are fixed
In happy copulation; if in evening mild, wearied with work,
Sit on a bank and draw the pleasures of this free–born joy.

The moment of desire! The moment of desire! The virgin
That pines for man shall awaken her womb to enormous joys
In the secret shadows of her chamber. The youth, shut up from
The lustful joy, shall forget to generate, and create an amorous image
In the shadows of his curtains and in the folds of his silent pillow.
Are not these the places of religion, the rewards of continence,
The self-enjoyings of self-denial? Why dost thou seek religion?

然後你以羞怯的處女之名聞之於世來掩飾自己，
用你在夜之枕下找到的網來獲取處女的歡樂，
並在上面打上「妓女」的烙印，在夜間把它
悄悄出賣，一聲不出，彷彿在睡夢中一樣。
神聖的夢和神聖的晚禱點燃了你煙騰騰的火焰：
你的熱情曾被誠實的黎明之眼點燃，
難道我的塞歐托曼追求羞怯的偽君子？
狡猾、機靈、隱祕、膽怯、謹慎、哆嗦的偽君子！

那麼奧松我就是妓女！而且生命的一切純潔的歡樂
都是妓女；那麼塞歐托曼就是個病人的夢；
奧松就是為自私的聖潔所役使的狡猾奴隸。

那不是奧松！奧松是個充滿了處女的幻想
向美常在之處的歡樂開放的處女。
我多想在旭日中找到那處所，我在快樂的交媾中
曾向那兒凝望；我多想在勞作之餘，
在溫暖的夜色中坐在岸邊，汲取這生來自由的歡悅。

慾望的時刻！慾望的時刻！為了男子
而憔悴的處女，將在臥室的隱祕暗影中把子宮
喚醒，來享受巨大的歡樂；禁戒肉慾之樂的青年
將把生育後代置諸腦後，在窗簾的暗影中、
在靜靜的眠枕的褶痕裡，臆造色情的影像。
難道這不正是宗教之所在，節慾之報償？
自我否定之自我欣賞？你為何尋求宗教？

Is it because acts are not lovely that thou seekest solitude,
Where the horrible darkness is impressed with reflections of desire?

Father of Jealousy, be thou accursed from the earth!
Why hast thou taught my Theotormon this accursed thing,
Till beauty fades from off my shoulders, darkened and cast out,
A solitary shadow wailing on the margin of nonentity?

I cry: Love! Love! Love! Happy, happy love, free as the mountain wind!
Can that be love that drinks another as a sponge drinks water,
That clouds with jealousy his nights, with weepings all the day,
To spin a web of age around him, grey and hoary, dark,
Till his eyes sicken at the fruit that hangs before his sight?
Such is self-love that envies all, a creeping skeleton,
With lamplike eyes watching around the frozen marriage bed.

But silken nets and traps of adamant will Oothoon spread,
And catch for thee girls of mild silver or of furious gold;
I'll lie beside thee on a bank and view their wanton play
In lovely copulation, bliss on bliss with Theotormon,
Red as the rosy morning, lustful as the first-born beam,
Oothoon shall view his dear delight, nor e'er with jealous cloud

尋求孤獨的行為難道有什麼可愛？
孤獨之處，那可怕的黑暗上印著慾望的影像！

嫉妒之父❷啊，受人世間的譴責吧！
你為何教我的塞歐托曼做這種可憎之事？
——要讓美從我雙肩凋落、暗淡，被拋出去，
形影相吊地嗚咽在虛無的邊緣。

我吶喊：愛！愛！幸福的愛幸福的愛！自由如同大風！
難道像海綿那樣只知道吸別人，能說是愛？
用嫉妒遮蔽自己的夜，用哭泣遮蔽整個白晝，
織出一張包圍自己生活的灰白而黑暗的網，
直到自己的眼睛厭惡掛在眼前的果實，能說是愛？
這樣的愛，是妒忌一切的自私的愛！是一條
眼睛睜得像燈一樣瘦骨伶仃、看守著婚床的爬虫。

奧松我將佈下絲織的羅網和剛玉的捕機，
為你捕捉柔亮如銀或剛烈似金的姑娘；
我將在河岸上躺在你身旁，看她們這些蕩婦
和你塞歐托曼一同遊戲在愛的交媾中，狂喜無度。
奧松我將紅艷如玫瑰的黎明，
貪慾似第一縷初升的光芒，

---

❷指上帝。

Come in the heaven of generous love, nor selfish blightings bring.

'Does the sun walk in glorious raiment on the secret floor
Where the cold miser spreads his gold? Or does the bright cloud drop
On his stone threshold? Does his eye behold the beam that brings
Expansion to the eye of pity? Or will he bind himself
Beside the ox to thy hard furrow? Does not that mild beam blot
The bat, the owl, the glowing tiger, and the king of night?
The sea-fowl takes the wintry blast for a covering to her limbs,
And the wild snake the pestilence to adorn him with gems and gold;
And trees and birds and beasts and men behold their eternal joy.
Arise, you little glancing wings, and sing your infant joy!
Arise and drink your bliss! For everything that lives is holy'

Thus every morning wails Oothoon. But Theotormon sits
Upon the margined ocean, conversing with shadows dire.

The daughters of Albion hear her woes, and echo back her sighs.

看著你熱切的歡樂,既不帶著嫉妒的陰雲
進入生育之愛的天空,也不會因自私而從事破壞。

難道太陽穿著輝煌的服裝漫步在隱秘的地板上,
看冷情的吝嗇鬼撒著金幣;難道燦爛的雲霞
漫遊在他的石頭門檻上?難道他的眼睛能看見
給憐憫之眼開拓眼界的光線;難道他會迫使自己在
母牛身旁踏著你堅硬的犁溝?難道那柔光未曾
點染蝙蝠、貓頭鷹、神采奕奕的虎和夜之王?
海鴨避入寒冷的疾風來遮蓋自己的身體;
兇野的蛇避入瘟疫中,用黃金和寶石來打扮自己;
樹木、禽、獸和人,看到自己永恆的歡愉。
升起吧,你小小的閃亮翅膀,歌唱你童稚的歡樂!
升起吧,暢飲你的狂喜,一切生物皆神聖!

每天黎明奧松都這樣慟哭,而塞歐托曼
坐在海洋的邊緣,在悲慘的陰影中變幻著。

阿爾比恩的女兒們聽到她的不幸,回應了她的嘆息。

1790-1793

The Marriage of Heaven and Hell

天國與地獄的婚姻

William Blake, *For Children: The Gates of Paradise*, object 14, 1793

The Argument

Rintrah roars and shakes his fires in the burdened air;
Hungry clouds swag on the deep.

Once meek, and in a perilous path,
The just man kept his course along
The vale of death.
Roses are planted where thorns grow,
And on the barren heath
Sing the honey bees.

Then the perilous path was planted;
And a river and a spring
On every cliff and tomb;
And on the bleached bones
Red clay brought forth.

Till the villain left the paths of ease,

引子❶

在沉悶的空中,林恰❷吼著,揮舞著火焰;
飢餓的陰影在大海上搖曳。

那正直的、曾經是溫順的人❸
沿著危險的小徑,沿著死亡之谷
一直走下去。
長滿荊棘之處長出了玫瑰,
荒蕪的、石南叢生的地方
蜜蜂在歌唱。

危險的小徑上也長出了玫瑰,
一條河與一泓泉水
流過一座座懸崖和墳墓;
一堆堆白骨
把紅土帶向前方。

那惡棍❹離開了舒坦的路,

---

❶引子中描寫的可能是《失樂園》一詩中亞當離開樂園後的情形。

❷布雷克的宗教體系中的神之一。

❸可能指亞當。

❹可能指米迦勒大天使。

To walk in perilous paths and drive
The just man into barren climes.

Now the sneaking serpent walks
In mild humility,
And the just man rages in the wilds
Where lions roam.

Rintrah roars and shakes his fires in the burdened air;
Hungry clouds swag on the deep.

As a new Heaven is begun, and it is now thirty-three years since its advent, the eternal Hell revives. And lo! Swedenborg is the angel sitting at the tomb; his writings are the linen clothes folded up. Now is the dominion of Edom, and the return of Adam into Paradise; see Isaiah XXXIV & XXXV chap:

    Without contraries is no progression. Attraction and repulsion, reason and energy, love and hate, are necessary to human existence.

    From these contraries spring what the religious call Good and Evil. Good is the passive that obeys reason: Evil is the active springing from energy.

    Good is heaven; Evil is Hell.

走上危險的小徑,他把正直的人
驅趕進不毛之地。

蹣跚的蛇❺,謙卑地
緩緩移動,
正直的人在野地裡大怒,
那裡獅子在漫步。

在沉悶的空中,林恰吼著,揮舞著火焰;
飢餓的陰影在大海上搖曳。

　　由於一個新天國的開始,且它已出現了三十三年,永恆的地獄復興了。看!坐在墳墓上的天使是斯威頓伯格❻:他的作品是折疊起來的亞麻衣服。現在是艾登在統治,是那回到伊甸園的亞當:見《以賽亞書》第三十四章和第三十五章❼。
　　離開對立面就沒有進步。吸引和排斥,理性和力,愛和恨,對人的生存都是必須的。
　　從這些對立面中產生了宗教所稱的善與惡,善是服從理性的被動的東西。惡是從力中產生的主動的東西。
　　善是天國,惡是地獄。

❺可能指魔王撒旦。

❻瑞典哲學家及宗教作家。

❼《以賽亞書》:《聖經》四大先知書之一;第三十四章和
　第三十五章為布雷克所杜撰。

The Voice of the Devil

All Bibles or sacred codes have been the causes of the following errors:
1. That man has two real existing principles, viz, a body and a soul.
2. That energy, called evil, is alone from the body, and that reason, called good, is alone from the soul.
3. That God will torment man in enternity for following his energies.

But the following contraries to these are true:
1. Man has no body distinct from his soul, for that called body is a protion of soul discerned by the five senses, the chief inlets of soul this age.
2. Energy is the only life and is from the body, and reason is the bound or outward circumference of energy.
3. Energy is eternal delight.

Those who restrain desire do so because theirs is weak enough to be restrained; and the restrainer or reason usurps its place and governs the unwilling.

And being restrained it by degrees becomes passive, till it is only the shadow of desire.

魔王的聲音

所有聖經和法典都成了下列錯誤的根源：

1. 人有兩個真正的生存本源，即：一個肉體和一個靈魂。
2. 力，叫做惡，僅來自肉體；而理性，叫做善，僅來自靈魂。
3. 上帝要永遠折磨人，因為人追隨他的力。

而這些錯誤的下列對立面卻是事實：
1. 人沒有相對靈魂而獨具的肉體；因為被叫做肉體的是靈魂中被五官感覺到的一部分，是這個時代靈魂的主要出口。
2. 力是唯一的生命，來自肉體，理性是力之界限或外圍。
3. 力是永恆的歡樂。

那些抑制慾望的人，之所以如此是因為其慾望脆弱，抑制得住；抑制者或者說理性侵佔了它的位置，統治了不情願的它。

由於受到抑制，它在某種程度上成了被動的東西，最終成為慾望的影子。

這段歷史記載在《失樂園》❽中，那統治者或

The history of this is written in *Paradise Lost,* and the governor (or reason) is called Messiah.

And the original archangel, or possessor of the command of the heavenly host, is called the Devil or Satan, and his children are called Sin and Death.

But in the *Book of Job,* Milton's Messiah is called Satan.

For this history has been adopted by both parties.

It indeed appeared to reason as if desire was cast out; but the Devil's account is that the Messiah fell, and formed a heaven of what he stole from the abyss.

This is shown in the Gospel, where he prays to the Father to send the comforter (or desire) that reason may have ideas to build on, the Jehovah of the Bible being no other than he who dwells in flaming fire. Know that after Christ's death he became Jehovah.

But in Milton the Father is destiny, the son a ration of the five senses, and the Holy Ghost vacuum!

Note. The reason Milton wrote in fetters when he wrote of angels and God, and at liberty when of Devils and Hell, is because he was a true poet, and of the Devil's party without knowing it.

者說理性叫做彌賽亞❾。

最早的天使長，或者說天軍統帥地位的佔有者，叫做魔王或撒旦，他的孩子叫做罪孽和死神。

但在《約伯記》❿中，彌爾頓的彌賽亞被稱為撒旦⓫。

因為這段歷史已為雙方所採納。

其實在理性面前，慾望似乎已被拋棄了；但魔王的價值在於：彌賽亞倒下去了，用他從地獄偷來的東西構造了一個天國。

對此，《福音書》講得很清楚。書中說，他祈求父親送來安慰⓬，或者說慾望，使理性得以依賴思想，因為《聖經》上的耶和華與居住在熊熊烈火中的他⓭並非二人。

要知道基督死後變成了耶和華。

但在彌爾頓看來，父親是命運，兒子是五官之比，是神聖空無！

旁白：彌爾頓以鐐銬來描寫天使和上帝，而以自由來描寫魔鬼和地獄。這是因為他是個真正的詩人，他不自覺地站在魔鬼一邊。

---

❽英國著名作家和詩人彌爾頓的傑作。

❾救難者之意，耶穌的稱號。

❿《舊約聖經》詩歌智慧書之一。

⓫意即《聖經》中的魔王是彌爾頓心中的救難者、救世主。

⓬雙關義，亦指聖靈。

⓭指魔王撒旦。

A Memorable Fancy

As I was walking among the fires of Hell, delighted with the enjoyments of genius (which to angels look like torment and insanity), I collected some of their proverbs, thinking that, as the sayings used in a nation mark its character, so the proverbs of Hell show the nature of infernal wisdom better than any description of buildings or garments.

When I came home, on the abyss of the five senses, where a flat-sided steep frowns over the present world, I saw a mighty devil folded in black clouds, hovering on the sides of the rock. With corroding fires he wrote the following sentence now perceived by the minds of men, and read by them on earth:

How do you know but every bird that cuts the airy way
Is an immense world of delight, closed by hour senses five?

Proverbs of Hell

In seed time learn, in harvest teach, in winter enjoy.
Drive your cart and your plough over the bones of the dead.
The road of excess leads to the palace of wisdom.

一個難忘的幻象

我在地獄之中漫遊,享受著在天使們看來是痛苦和瘋狂的樂趣的時候,曾蒐集了一些箴言。我想,正如各種諺語常標誌著一個民族的特徵一樣,地獄的箴言也表現了地獄的智慧之本性,且比任何對地獄中的建築和衣著的描述更能說明問題。

我回家的時候,在五官的深淵上,有一齊塹的峭壁對現世表示著不滿。我看見一罩在烏雲中的高大魔鬼,在岩壁旁飛來飛去,用腐蝕之火寫下現在已為人們的思想所接受、且在人世間廣泛流傳的下列語句:

你如何知道展翅橫空的每一隻鳥兒
是你的五官所包容的、無邊的歡樂世界?

地獄的箴言

播種時節學習,收穫時節教誨,冬天享樂。
在屍骨上駛過你的馬車和犁。

Prudence is a rich ugly old maid courted by incapacity.

He who desires but acts not breeds pestilence.

The cut worm forgives the plough.

Dip him in the river who loves water.

A fool sees not the same tree that a wise man sees.

He whose face gives no light shall never become a star.

Eternity is in love with the productions of Time.

The busy bee has no time for sorrow.

The hours of folly are measured by the clock, but of wisdom no clock can measure.

All wholesome food is caught without a net or a trap.

Bring out number, weight and measure in a year of dearth.

No bird soars too high, if he soars with his own wings.

A dead body revenges not injuries.

The most sublime act is to set another before you.

If the fool would persist in his folly he would become wise.

Folly is the cloak of Knavery.

Shame is Pride's cloak.

Prisons are built with stones of Law, brothels with bricks of Religion.

The pride of the peacock is the glory of God.

The lust of the goat is the bounty of God.

The wrath of the lion is the wisdom of God.

The nakedness of woman is the work of God.

Excess of sorrow laughs. Excess of joy weeps.

The roaring of lions, the howling of wolves, the raging of the stormy sea, and the destructive sword are por-tions of eternity too great

超脫之路通往智慧之境。
節儉是無能所追求的一個富有而醜陋的老處女。
有所慾求而無所行動,就會滋生邪念。
被切斷的蚯蚓原諒犁。
把好玩水者浸到水中。
傻瓜看不到聰明人所看到的樹。
臉上不放光的人,永遠不會變成星星。
永恆寓於愛之中,帶著時間的成果。
忙碌的蜜蜂沒有時間去悲傷。
愚蠢的鐘點用時鐘來計數,智慧的鐘點則是時鐘所不能計算的。
一切潔淨的食物都不是用漁網或獵夾獲取的。
從死去的歲月中產生數字、重量和長度。
只靠自己的翅膀飛翔的鳥兒,不會飛得太高。
死屍不報復他人的傷害。
最崇高的行為是先人後己。
傻瓜若堅持自己的愚蠢,就會變得聰明起來。
愚蠢是無賴的偽裝。
羞愧是驕傲的偽裝。
監獄用律法之石建造,妓院用宗教之磚砌成。
孔雀的驕傲是上帝的光榮。
山羊的淫慾❹是上帝的慷慨。
獅子的憤怒是上帝的智慧。
女人的裸體是上帝的傑作。

---

❹在古希臘神話中,山羊象徵淫慾。

for the eye of man.
The fox condemns the trap, not himself.
Joys impregnate. Sorrows bring forth.
Let man wear the fell of the lion, woman the fleece of the sheep.
The bird a nest, the spider a web, man friendship.
The selfish smiling fool and the sullen frowning fool shall be both thought wise, that they may be a rod.
What is now proved was once only imagined.
The rat, the mouse, the fox, the rabbit, watch the roots. Tho lion, the tiger, the horse, the elephant, watch the fruits.
The cistern contains: the fountain overflows.
One thought fills immensity.
Always be ready to speak your mind, and a base man will avoid you.
Everything possible to be believed is an image of truth.
The eagle never lost so much time as when he submitted to learn of the crow.
The fox provides for himself, but God provides for the lion.
Think in the morning. Act in the noon. Eat in the evening. Sleep in the night.
He who has suffered you to impose on him, knows you.
As the plough follows words, so God rewards prayers.
The tigers of wrath are wiser than the horses of instruction.
Expect posion from the standing water.
You never know what is enough unless you know what is more than enough.
Listen to the fool's reproach: it is a kingly title.

悲極生樂，樂極生悲。
獅吼、狼嚎、暴風雨中海洋的洶湧和毀滅性的殺戮，是永恆的幾個部分，它們在人的眼睛看來是太偉大了。
狐狸責備陷阱，而不責備自己。
歡樂滿了，悲傷來了。
讓男人披上獅皮，讓女人披上羊毛。
鳥兒靠的是巢，蜘蛛靠的是網，人靠的是友誼。
自私這微笑的傻瓜，慍怒這皺眉的傻瓜，都該被視為聰明，它們可能成為權杖。
現在得到證實的事情曾經只是幻想。
耗子、老鼠、狐狸和野兔，注意到塊根；獅子、老虎、馬兒和大象，注意到果子。
池水不動，泉水流湧。
單一的思想充滿了無限。
時刻準備說出你的想法，則一個卑鄙的人就會迴避你。
每一件可信的事物都是真理的映像。
鷹在被迫學雞叫時最浪費時間。
狐狸供養自己，而上帝供養獅子。
早晨思考，中午行動，傍晚用餐，夜間睡眠。
受過你欺騙的人，了解你。（或：容忍過你強加於他的人，了解你）
當犁跟隨諾言時，上帝酬答禱告者。
遭過天譴的虎比有過教訓的馬更聰明。
止水生毒。

The eyes of fire, the nostrils of air, the mouth of water, the beard of earth.

The weak in courage is strong in cunning.

The apple tree never asks the beech how he shall grow, nor the lion the horse, how he shall take his prey.

The thankful receiver bears a plentiful harvest.

If others had not been foolish, we should be so.

The soul of sweet delight can never be defiled.

When thou seest an eagle, thou seest a portion of genius lift up thy head!

As the caterpillar chooses the fairest leaves to lay her eggs on, so the priest lays his curse on the fairest joys.

To create a little flower is the loabour of ages.

Damn braces. Bless relaxes.

The best wine is the oldest. The best water the newest.

Prayers plough not. Praises reap not.

Joys laugh not! Sorrows weep not!

The head Sublime, the heart Pathos, the genitals Beauty, the hands and feet Proportion.

As the air to a bird or the sea to a fish, so is contempt to the contemptible.

The crow wished everything was black; the owl, that everything was white.

Exuberance is beauty.

If the lion was advised by the fox, he would be cunning.

Improvement makes straight roads, but the crooked roads without

你不會知道什麼是滿足，除非你知道什麼超過滿足。

聽聽傻瓜的責備！這可是君王的權利！

眼睛由火構成，鼻子由空氣、嘴由水、鬍鬚由泥構成。

勇敢中的脆弱是狡猾中的強大。

蘋果樹決不會向山毛櫸請教怎樣生長，獅子也不會向馬請教如何捕獵。

感恩的受惠者產生豐盛的收獲。

如果別人沒有傻，那我們一定傻了。

有著美妙的歡樂的靈魂絕不會被玷污。

當你看到一隻鷹的時候，你就看到了天才的一部分：抬起你的頭來！

正如毛蟲選擇最美麗的葉子來產卵一樣，神父選擇最美妙的歡樂來詛咒。

創造一朵小花須花費相當長時間的勞動。

詛咒使人振奮，祝福使人鬆懈。

酒越陳越香，水越新越甜。

祈禱不能代替耕作！讚美不會給你收獲！

真正的歡樂不笑！真正的悲傷不哭！（或：真喜不笑，真悲不哭）

頭在於崇高，心在於憐憫，性徵在於美，手腳在於勻稱。

輕蔑之於卑鄙正如空氣之於鳥，水之於魚。

烏鴉希望一切是黑的，夜鴉希望一切是白的。

生機勃勃就是美。

improvement are roads of Genius.
Sooner murder an infant in its cradle than nurse unacted diesires.
Where man is not, nature is barren.
Truth can never be told so as to be understood and not be believed.
Enough, or too much!

    The ancient poets animated all sensible objects with gods or geniuses, callling them by the names, and adorning them with the prpoerties of woods, rivers, mountains, lakes, cities, nations, and whatever their enlarged and numerous senses could perceive.

    And particularly they studied the genius of each city and country, placing it under its mental deity.

    Till a system was formed, which some took advantage of, and enslaved the vulgar by attempting to realise or abstract the mental deities from their objects. Thus began priesthood–choosing forms of worship from poetic tales.

    And at length they pronounced that the gods had ordered such things.

    Thus men forgot that all deities reside in the human breast.

獅子聽了狐狸的勸告，就會變得狡詐。

改良帶來了筆直的道路，但未獲改良的彎曲小路是天才之路。

把嬰兒扼死在搖籃裡，是未經思索的行為。

無人之處，大自然荒蕪。

真理容易理解，不易言傳，難以置信。

夠了！或許太多了。

從前的詩人，用神和天才來把一切易感的事物描繪得栩栩如生，用名字來稱呼這些事物，用樹林、河流、山巒、湖泊、城市、民族，以及一切能為他們的延伸了的感官所領悟的事物的特性來使之生色。

尤其是他們研究了各個城市和鄉村的風尚，將它們歸於其內在的神性。

這些努力一直進行到一個體系的建立為止，這個體系大約有某些優點，且企圖通過從客觀事實中顯現或抽象出內在的神性來征服粗俗：於是開始有了教士的職業——

接著從詩體傳說中選擇了崇拜的形象。

最後他們宣稱神主宰了一切。

這樣，人們就忘了所有的神都居住於人的胸中。

A Memorable Fancy

The prophets Isaiah and Ezekiel dined with me, and I asked them how they dared so roundly to asset that God spoke to them; and whether they did not think at the time that they would be misunderstood, and so be the cause of imposition.

Isaish answered, 'I saw no God, nor heard any, in a finite organical perception; but my senses discovered the infinite in everything, and as I was then persuaded, and remain confirmed, that the voice of honest indignation is the voice of God, I cared not for consequences, but wrote.'

Then I asked: 'Does a firm persuasion that a thing is so, make it so?'

He replied, 'All poets believe that it does, and in ages of imagination the firm persuasion removed mountains; but many are not capable of a firm persuasion of anything.'

Then Ezekiel said, 'The philosophy of the east taught the first principles of human percepitons; some nations held one principle for the origin and some another. We of Israel taught that the Poetic Genius (as you now call it) was the first principle, and all the others merely de-rivative—which was the cause of our despising the priests

一個難忘的幻象

先知以賽亞和以西結和我一起進餐,我問他們怎敢直言不諱堅持上帝告訴他們的一切;當時他們曾否想到,他們會受到誤解,從而成為欺詐的根源。

以賽亞答道:「以有限的器官的感覺,我沒有看見過也沒有聽見過上帝;但我的感官發現了一切中的無限,於是我被征服了,繼而堅信真正的憤慨之聲是上帝的聲音,我未曾關心結論,而是寫下了它們。」

於是我問道:「是不是『某件事是如此』這樣一個堅定的信念,使那件事如此呢?」

他答道:「所有詩人都相信這一點,且相信在想像的時代,這堅定的信念曾移動了大山;但許多人都沒有堅信某件事的本領。」

以西結接著說道:「東方哲學道出了人類知覺的第一原則:對於起源問題,一些民族堅持一種原則,另一些則堅持另一種:我們教導以色列人說,詩的本質(正如你們現在所言)是第一原則:其他一切幾乎都是派生出來的,由此緣故,我們輕視了其他國家的神父和哲學家,並且,預言所有神最終

and philosophers of other countries, and prophesying that all gods would at last be proved to originate in ours and to be the tributaries of the Poetic Genius. It was this that our great poet, King David, desired so fervently and invoked so pathetically, saying by this he conquers enemies and governs knigdoms. And we so loved our God, that we cursed in his name all the deities of surrounding nations, and asserted that they had rebelled; from these opinions the vulgar came to think that all nations would at last be subject to the Jews.

'This,' said he, 'like all firm persuasions, is come to pass, for all nations believe the Jews' code and worship the Jews' God, and what greater subjection can be?'

I heard this with some wonder, and must confess my own conviction. After dinner I asked Isaiah to favour the world with his lost works; he said none of equal value was lost. Ezekiel said the same of his.

I also asked Isaiah what made him go naked and barefoot for three years. He answered, 'The same that made our firend Diogenes the Grecian.'

I then asked Ezekiel why he ate dung; and lay so long on his right and left side. He answered, 'The desire of raising other men into a perception of the infinite: This the North American tribes practise, and is he honest who resists his genius or conscience only for the sake of present ease or gratification?'

將被證明起源於我們的神,且從屬於詩的本質:我們的偉大詩人大衛王曾熱切想望和哀婉懇求的正是這一點。我們說,他正是用這一點征服了敵人並統治了王國;我們太熱愛我們的上帝,竟用他的名義來詛咒周圍各民族的神,並且宣稱他們是叛逆:從這些觀點出發,粗俗的人最終認為各民族將從屬於猶太人。」

「這一點,」他說:「像所有堅定的信仰一樣,已經得到實現;因為所有民族都相信猶太法典,崇拜猶太人的神,難道還有比這更大的服從嗎?」

我有些驚奇地聽著,必須坦白,我自己是深信不疑的。午餐後,我請求他,把失傳的著作賜給人世;他說沒有失傳有價值的著作。以西結也如是說。

我又問以賽亞,是什麼原因使他赤足裸身三年?他答道:「是促使我們的朋友希臘人狄俄吉尼苦行的同一個原因。」

接著我問以賽亞,他為何食糞和長時間地側身躺著?他答道:「是因為喚起別人進入無限知覺的願望:這在北美部落是常有的事,為了眼下安逸的緣故而與自己的天才或良心作對,這種人難道正直可敬嗎?」

The ancient tradition that the world will be consumed in fire at the end of six thousand years is true, as I have heard from Hell.

For the cherub with his flaming sword is hereby commanded to leave his guard at Tree of Life; and when he does, the whole creation will be consumed, and appear infinite and holy, whereas it now appears finite and corrupt.

This will come to pass by an improvement of sensual enjoyment.

But first the notion that man has a body distince from his soul is to be expunged. This I shall do by printing in the infernal method by corrosives, which in Hell are salutary and medicinal, melting apparent surfaces away, and displaying the infinite which was hid.

If the doors of perception were cleansed everything would appear to man as it is–infinite.
For man has closed himself up, till he sees all things through narrow chinks of his cavern.

在六千年之末這世界將在火焰中毀滅的古老傳說是真的,就像我在地獄中聽説的那樣。

因為帶著燃燒的箭的小天使將受命離開他在生命之樹❶⓹旁的崗位,一旦他離開,所有的創造物❶⓺都將毀滅而顯現出無限與神聖,而現在顯現的是有限和腐朽。

這將隨著感官享樂的改善而得到實現。

但首先,人有一個相對於靈魂而獨具的肉體這樣一個概念必須清除掉;我解決這個問題的方法,是用冥界的辦法打上印記,即通過腐蝕——地獄裡的補品和醫藥——來融去外表,顯示出隱藏著的無限。

一旦知覺之門打掃清潔,一切都會向人顯示出本相——無限。

這是因為人把自身封閉起來了,要等到他通過他的洞的窄縫看見一切為止。

---

❶⓹《聖經》說,亞當和夏娃吃了智慧之樹上的禁果,但幸虧沒有碰生命之樹,否則人不但有了智慧,而且能永生。

❶⓺上帝所創造的天地萬物。

A Memorable Fancy

I was in a printing-house in Hell, and saw the method in which knowledge is transmitted from generation to generation.

In the first chamber was a dragon-man, clearing away the rubbish from a cave's month; within, a number of dragons were hollowing the cave.

In the second chamber was a viper folding round the rock and the cave, and others adorning it with gold, silver and precious stones.

In the third chamber was an eagle with wings and feathers of air; he caused the inside of the cave to be in- finite. Around were numbers of eagle-like men, who built palaces in the immense cliffs.

In the foruth chamber were lions of flaming fire, raging around and melting the metals into living fluids.

In the fifth chamber were unnamed forms, which cast the metals into the expanse.

There they were received by men who occupied the sixth chamber, and took the forms of books and were arranged in libraries.

The giants who formed this world into its sensual existence, and now seem to live in it in chains, are in truth the causes of its life and the sources of all activity; but the chains are the cunning

一個難忘的幻象

我在地獄的印刷廠裡，看到知識一代一代流傳的方法。

第一個房間裡是一個龍人，他在清除一個洞口的垃圾：裡面有幾個人在挖洞。

第二個房間裡是一條蟒蛇，他盤在岩石和洞口上，其餘的在用黃金、白銀和大理石裝飾他。

第三個房間裡是一隻鷹，他長著翅膀和飛翔的羽翎：他使洞的內部變得無限。他周圍是幾個像人一樣的鷹，他們在巨大的峭壁上建造宮殿。

第四個房間是燃著熊熊的火焰的獅子，他四處狂奔著，將金屬熔化成生命之液。

第五個房間裡是無名物，他在把金屬拋進瀚海裡。

它們為占有第六室的人所接收，這些人使書成型，並使之陳列在藏書室裡。

使這世界形成肉感的實體、現在似乎戴著鎖鏈生活在這世界上的巨人，確實是世界的生命及一切活動的根源；但那鎖鏈是馴服的頭腦中的狡詐，它有能力抗拒力；據箴言說：勇敢中的脆弱在狡詐時是強大的。

那麼生存的一部分就是創造力的富有；另一個部分則是貪婪：在貪婪者看來，創造者似乎戴著鎖鏈；但並非如此，貪婪者僅僅取得了存在的幾個部

of weak and tame minds, which have power to resist energy. According to the proverb, 'the weak in courage is strong in cunning.'

Thus one portion of being is the Prolific, the other, the Devouring. To the devourer it seems as if the producer was in his chains, but it is not so; he only takes protions of existence and fancies that the whole.

But the prolific would cease to be prolific unless the devourer, as a sea, received the excess of his delights.

Some will say, 'Is not God alone the Prolific?' I answer, 'God only acts and is in existing beings or men.' These two classes of men are always upon earth, and they should be enemies: whoever tries to reconcile them seeks to destroy existence.

Religion is an endeavour to reconcile the two.

Note. Jesus Christ did not wish to unite but to separate them, as in the parable of sheep and goats. And he says, 'I came not to send peace, but a sword.'

Messiah or Satan or Tempter was formerly thought to be one of the Antediluvians who are our energies.

A Memorable Fancy

An angel came to me and said, 'O pitiable, foolish young man! O horrible! O dreadful state! Consider the hot burning dungeon thou art preparing for thyself to all

分，而他把那幻想成了整體。

除非貪婪者像海洋一樣容納創造力的富有的過度的歡樂，後者將不再富有創造力。

有人會說：「難道上帝不僅是創造力的富有嗎？」我的回答是：「上帝僅行動並存在於生存者或者說人的身上。」

這兩類人永遠在世界上，他們應是敵人：無論誰試圖和解他們都是試圖消滅存在。

宗教是和解他們的一個努力。

旁白：耶穌基督並未曾想合併他們，他是想分開他們的，比如在綿羊和山羊的比喻中！他說：「我不是來送和平，而是來送刀劍。」

彌賽亞或者說撒旦或者說誘惑者，從前被視為大洪水之前的人們中的一個，他是我們的力。

一個難忘的幻象

一個天使向我走來，並且說道：「多可憐啊，愚蠢的年輕人！啊，真讓人毛骨悚然！啊，可怕的國家！想想你正替自己為整個永恆所準備的灼灼燃

eternity, to which thou art going in such a career.'

I said: 'Perhaps you will be willing to show me my eternal lot, and we will contemplate together upon it, and see whether your lot or mine is most desirable.'

So he took me through a stable and through a church and down into the church vault, at the end of which was a mill. Through the mill we went, and came to a cave; down the winding cavern we groped our tedious way, till a void boundless as a nether sky appeared beneath us, and we held by the roots of trees and hung over this immensity. But I said, 'If you please we will commit ourselves to this void, and see whether providence is here also; if you will not, I will.' But he answered, 'Do not presume, O young man, but as we here remain, behold thy lot which will soon appear when the darkness passes away.'

So I remained with him sitting in the twisted root of an oak. He was suspended in a fungus which hung with the head downward into the deep.

By degrees we beheld the infinite abyss, fiery as the smoke of a burning city; beneath us at an immense distance was the sun, black but shining. Round it were fiery tracks on which revolved vast spiders, crawling after their prey, which flew or rather swum, in the infinite deep, in the most terrific shapes of animals sprung from corruption; and the air was full or them, and seemed composed of them: these are devils, and are called

燒的土牢,為了它你陷入如此的憂心之中。」

我說道:「也許你願意向我顯示我的永恒的命運,我們將一同為此冥思苦想,看看你我的命運是否是最稱心的。」

於是他帶我穿過馬廄,教堂,下到教堂的墓穴裡。這墓穴的末端是一個磨坊,我們穿過磨坊,來到一個洞中:我們下到洞裡,摸索地走了很長一段路,最後,我們下面出現了好像一片地下天空似的茫茫空間。我們抓著樹根,懸在這無限的空間之上,我說道:「如果你願意,我們不妨把自己交給這空間,看看這兒是否也有天命:我願意這樣做,但你願意嗎?」他答道:「別放肆,年輕人啊,還是像我們現在這樣的好,看你的命運吧,不久,黑暗隱去之時它就會顯現。」

我就仍和他在一起,我坐在一棵橡樹的蟠蚪的樹根之中:他則吊在一根傘菌上,那棵傘菌伸入深空,頭朝下懸著。

漸漸地,我們看清了那無限的深淵,它像一個燃燒的城市的煙柱一樣冒著火焰;我們下面極遠的地方是那太陽,它是黑的,然而放著光:它周圍是燃燒著的航跡,航跡上盤旋著巨大的蜘蛛。他們在獵物後面爬行,那些獵物飛走了,或者不如說飄走了,飄進了無垠的深空,其狀如同從腐物中跳出的動物,極為可怕;他們布滿空中,彷彿天空就是由他們所構成:這些是魔鬼,叫做空中之神。我問同伴,何者是我的命運?他說:「在黑蜘蛛與白蜘蛛

Powers of the Air. I now asked my companion which was my eternal lot; he said, 'Between the black and white spiders.'

But now, from between teh black and white spiders, a cloud and fire burst and rolled through the deep, blackening all beneath, so that the nether deep grew black as a sea, and rolled with a terrible noise. Beneath us was nothing now to be seen but a black tempest, till looking east between the clouds and the waves, we saw a cataract of blood mixed with fire; and not many stones' throw from us appeared and sunk again the scaly fold of a monstrous serpent. At last, to the east, distant about three degrees, appeared a fiery crest above the waves; slowly it reared like a ridge of golden rocks, till we discovered two globes of cirmson fire, form which the sea fled away in clouds of smoke; and now we saw it was the head of Leviathan. His forehead was divided into streaks of green and purple like those on a tiger's forehead; soon we saw his mouth and red gills hang just above the raging foam, tinging the black deep with beams of blood, advancing toward us with all the fury of a spiritual existence.

My friend the angel climbed up from his station into the mill. I remained alone, and then this appearance was no more, but I found myself sitting on a pleasant bank beside a river by moonlight, hearing a harper who sung to the harp; and his theme was, 'The man who never alters his opinion is like

之間。」

　而此時,白蜘蛛和黑蜘蛛中間是一片火雲,它燃燒著,翻滾著穿過深空,使下方一片黑暗。於是那地下的深空變得漆黑如海,滾過一陣可怕的聲音:除了一陣黑色的風暴,下面什麼也看不見。終於,當我們向雲與波浪之間眺望東方時,看見了一條冒著火焰的血瀑布,且看見我們所拋出的不多幾塊石頭浮現而又沉沒在一條怪蛇的鱗甲的褶皺中:最後,在偏東三度遠的地方,在波浪上出現了一個火紅的波峰:它像一個金色岩石組成的山脊一樣緩緩豎起。接著我們發現了兩個緋紅的火球,海洋離它們而去,消失在煙雲之中;這時我們看出,它是海中怪獸列維坦❼的頭部;牠的前額分成綠紫相間的條紋,就像虎額上的條紋一樣:不久我們便看到了牠的嘴和紅色的顎垂肉,牠懸在翻騰的泡沫的正上方,用血光染著深空,以一個精靈之實體的全部狂怒向我們推進。

　我的天使朋友從他的落腳處爬進了磨坊;我獨自留在那裡,那影像卻驀然間消失無蹤了;我發現自己坐在一條河的令人怡悅的河岸上,月光照著我,一個彈豎琴的人在邊彈邊唱,他唱的是:「誰從不改變自己的觀點,誰就好比一潭死水,他的思想上就會長出爬蟲。」

　但是我站起身來去找那個磨坊了,在磨坊中我

---

❼Levitan:《聖經》中提到的怪獸。

standing water, and breeds reptiles of the mind.'

But I arose, and sought for the mill, and there I found my angel, who, surpirsed, asked me how I escaped?

I answered, 'All that we saw was owing to your metaphysics; for when you ran away, I found myself on a bank by moonlight hearing a harper. But now we have seen my eternal lot, shall I show you yours?' He laughed at my proposal; but I, by force suddenly caught him in my arms, and flew westerly through the night, till we were elevated above the earth's shadow. Then I flung myself with him directly into the body of the sun. Here I clothed myself in white, and taking in my hand Swedenborg's volumes, sunk from the glorious clime, and passed all the planets till we came to Saturn. Here I stayed to rest, and then leaped into the void between Saturn and the fixed stars.

'Here,' said I, 'is your lot, in this space, if space it may be called.' Soon we saw the stable and the church, and I took him to the altar and opened the Bible, and lo! it was a deep pit, into which I descended, driving the angel before me. Soon we saw seven hourses of brick, one we entered; in it were a number of monkeys, baboons, and all of that species, chained by the middle, grinning and snatching at one another, but withheld by the shortness of their chains. However I saw that they sometimes grew numerous, and then the weak were caught by the strong and with a grinning aspect, first coupled with, and then devoured, by plucking off first one limb and then another till the body was left a helpless trunk. This, after grinning and

找到了我的天使,他驚奇地問我是怎樣逃脫的?

我答道:「我們所見的一切都歸功於你的玄學;因為你走開時,我發現自己在河岸上,沐著月光聽著豎琴,但現在既已見到我的永恆的命運,你要我也把你的顯示出來嗎?」祂對我的建議付之一笑;而我卻突然憑著氣力用手臂抓住了他,穿過黑夜向西飛去,一直飛到大地之蔭的上空;然後,我把他和我自己一同拋入了太陽體內;這時,我身穿白衣,手中拿著斯威頓伯格的書,從那輝煌的所在下沉,經過了所有的行星,最後來到土星上:這時,我停下來休息了一刻,然後躍入了土星與恆星之間的空間。

「這兒,」我說,「是你的命運;它在這太空裡,如果這兒可稱為太空的話。」不久,我們看到了馬廄和教堂,我把他帶往祭壇,打開了《聖經》。看!它是個深深的地洞。我走了進去,一面推著我前面的天使,一面在洞中下降:不久,我們看到了七間磚房:我們走進了其中的一間,看到裡面是幾隻猴子、狒狒和所有那一類的動物,他們被攔腰鏈著,互相咧嘴,互相抓撓,但是又因為鏈子短而受到阻礙:可是,我看到他們有時一大群撕打起來。於是,弱者被強者抓住,咧著嘴露出了痛苦的樣子,他先被交配,繼而被一隻肢子一隻肢子地撕食了,最後只剩下一具孤零零的軀幹:就連這軀幹,撕食者在假惺惺地向它咧咧嘴,親親它以後,也把它吞吃了;到處我都看到有那麼一隻猴子在饒有興味地

kissing it with seeming fondness, they devoured too; and here and there I saw one savourily picking the flesh off of his own tail; as the stench terribly annoyed us both, we sent into the mill, and I in my hand brought the skeleton of a body, which in the mill was Aristotle's *Analytics*.

So the angel said:'Thy fantasy has imposed upon me and thou oughtest to be ashamed.'

I answered: 'We impose on one another, and it is but lost time to converse with you whose works are only Analytics.' Opposition is True Friendship.

I have always found that angels have the vanity to speak of themselves as the only wise; they do with a confident insolence sprouting from systematic reasoning.

Thus Swedenborg boasts that what he writes is new, though it is only the contents or index of already- published books.

A man carried a monkey about for a show, and because he was a little wiser than the monkey, grew vain, and conceived himself as much wiser than seven men. It is so with Swedenborg: he shows the folly of churches and exposes hypocrites, till he imagines that all are religious, and himself the single one on earth that ever broke a net.

Now hear a plain fact: Swedengorg has not written one new truth. Now hear another: he has written all the old falsehoods.

And now hear the reason. He conversed with angels, who are all religious, and conversed not with devils who all hate religion,

撕下自己尾巴上的肉：那種惡臭使我們倆都厭煩極了，我們就走進了磨坊。我用手帶走了磨坊裡一具屍骸的骷髏，它是亞里多德的《邏輯分析方法》。

因此那天使說道：「你的怪念頭欺騙了我，你應該感到羞恥。」

我答道：「我們在互相欺騙，和你交談只是浪費時間，你的著作不過是《邏輯分析方法》。」真正的友誼是對立。

我已時常發現，天使們有虛榮心，這使他們把自己說成唯一聰明的人：他們就帶著自負的蠻橫態度，根據系統性的推理侃侃而談。

斯威頓伯格就這樣自誇所寫的東西是新穎的東西，儘管它們只是已經出版的書籍中的目錄或索引。

一個人帶著一隻獅子大概是為了炫耀自己，僅僅因為自己比猴子聰明那麼一丁點兒，就變得自負起來，以為自己的智慧比七個人的智慧還多。斯威頓伯格就是這樣：他表現了教會的愚蠢，暴露了偽君子的面目，他甚至設想一切都是宗教，而他自己則是世界上唯一衝破羅網的人。

現在請聽一個顯然的事實：斯威頓勃格沒有寫下過一個新的真理。再請聽另一個事實：他寫下了所有陳腐的謊言。

現在請聽理由，他和天使們交談，這些天使全是修士，他又和魔鬼們交談，他們則全是仇恨宗教的。這是因為他沒有能圓通他的自負的想法。

for he was incapable through his conceited notions.

Thus Swedenborg's writings are a recapitulation of all superficial opinions and an analysis of the more sublime—but no further.

Have now another plain fact: any man of mechanical talents may, from the writings of Paracelsus or Jacob Behmen, produce ten thousand volumes of equal value with Swedenborg's, and from those of Dante or Shakespeare an infinite number.

But when he has done this, let him not say that he knows better than his master, for he only holds a candle in sunshine.

A Memorable Fancy

Once I saw a devil in a flame of fire, who arose before an angel that sat on a cloud; and the devil uttered these words: 'The worship of God is: Honouring his gifts in other men, each according to his genius, and loving the greatest men best: those who envy or calumniate great men hate God, for there is no other God.'

The angel, hearing this, became almost blue, but mastering himself he grew yellow, and at last white, pink and smiling, and then replied:

'Thou idolater, is not God One? and is he not visible in Jesus

所以，斯威頓伯格的著作是一些膚淺的觀點的簡單重述，是更極端——但不是更深刻的分析。

現在請看另一個顯然的事實：一切有機械的才能的人，都可以從柏拉圖或雅各、貝赫曼的著作之中，搞出和斯威頓伯格的著作具有同樣的價值的內容，從但丁或莎士比亞的著作中搞出無數的東西。

但既然他是這麼做的，就不要讓他說自己比大師們懂得更多，因為他只是在陽光之中拿著一支蠟燭。

一個難忘的幻象

有一次，我見到一個披著火焰的魔鬼，他出現在一位駕著雲的天使面前，說了這些話：
「對上帝的崇拜在於，依據各人的天賦，使自己的才能在別人身上得到榮耀，並且最愛偉大的人：那些嫉妒或誹謗偉人的人們仇恨上帝，因為沒有別的上帝。」

天使聽了，臉色幾乎發了青；但是他克制著自己，臉色變黃，最後變得蒼白又發紅，且微笑了，然後他答道：
「你這盲目的崇拜者：難道上帝不只一個？難道他

Christ? and has not Jesus Christ given his sanction to the law of ten commandments? and are not all other men fools, sinners, and nothings?'

The devil answered, 'Bray a fool in a mortar with wheat, yet shall not his folly be beaten out of him. If Jesus Christ is the greatest man, you ought to love him in the greatest degree. Now hear how he has given his sanction to the law of ten commandments: did he not mock at the Sabbath, and so mock the Sabbath's God? Murder those who were murdered because of him? Turn away the law from the woman taken in adultery? Steal the labour of others to support him? Bear false witness when he omitted making a defence before Pilate? Covet when he prayed for his disciples, and when he bid them shake off the dust of their feet against such as refused to lodge them? I tell you, no virtue can exist without breaking these ten commandments. Jesus was all virtue, and acted from impulse, not from rules.'

When he had so spoken I beheld the angel who stretched out his arms, embracing the flame of fire, and he was consumed and arose as Elijah.

Note. This angel, who is now become a devil, is my particular friend. We often read the Bible together in its infernal or

在耶穌基督身上不可以見到?難道耶穌基督沒有讚許十誡?難道其餘一切人不都是傻瓜、罪人和微不足道的人?」

魔鬼答道:「把一個傻瓜和小麥一起放在臼裡搗碎,也不會把他的愚蠢搗出來。如果耶穌基督是偉大的人,你就該愛他最深:現在請聽他是怎樣對十誡加以讚許的:難道他沒有嘲笑安息日,從而嘲笑了安息日的上帝?難道他沒有使律法對通姦的婦女避而不視?難道他沒有竊取別人的勞動來供養自己?當他在皮雷特[18]面前忘了作出答辯的時候,難道他不是提供了偽證?當他為他的門徒祈禱的時候,難道他沒有過妄想?當他吩咐他們抖腳上的塵土時,難道他沒有顯得好像要拒絕接受他們[19]?我告訴你,沒有美德能不破這十誡而存在。耶穌是完全的美德。他行動是出於刺激,而不是出於準則。」

他這樣說的時候,我注視著天使,那天使伸出臂膀擁抱那火焰[20],他被燒毀了,且像以利亞一樣得到了復活。

旁白:這位天使現在已變成了一個魔鬼,他是我特殊的朋友:我們常在一起讀《聖經》,讀它的地

---

[18] 疑為彼拉多之誤。彼拉多,巡撫,耶穌被判死刑後交給他,他向耶穌問話,耶穌不答。

[19] 以上列舉的耶穌行為,在《聖經》中均有褒揚性質的敘述。

[20] 指魔鬼。

diabolical sense, which the world shall have if they behave well.

I have also The Bible of Hell, which the world shall have whether they will or no.

One Law for the Lion and Ox is Oppression.

獄或惡魔的道理,這一些,行為好的世人可以讀到。

我也有地獄的《聖經》,這《聖經》世人都有,不管他要不要。

一條約束獅子和牛的律法叫壓迫。

1792

A Song of Liberty

自由之歌

William Blake, *For Children: The Gates of Paradise*, object 9, 1793

1. The Eternal Female groand! It is heard over all the Earth.
2. Albion's coast is sick, silent; the American meadows faint!
3. Shadows of Prophecy shiver along by the lakes and the rivers and mutter across the ocean. France, rend down thy dungeon!
4. Golden Spain, burs the barriers of old Rome!
5. Cast thy keys, O Rome, into the deep down falling, even to eternity down falling,
6. And weep.
7. In her trembling hands she took the new born terror, howling.
8. On those infinite mountains of light now barr'd out by the Atlantic sea, the new born fire stood before the starry ing!
9. Flag'd with grey brow'd snows and thunderous visages, the jealous wings wav'd over the deep.
10. The speary hand burned aloft, unbuckled was the shield, forth went the hand of jealousy among the flaming hair, and hurl'd the new born wonder thro' the starry night.
11. The fire, the fire, is falling!
12. Look up! look up! O citizen of London, enlarge thy countenance! O Jew, leave counting gold! return to thy oil and wine. O African! black African! (Go, winged thought, widen his forehead.)
13. The fiery limbs, the flaming hair, shot like the sinking sun into the western sea.

1. 永恆的女性在嘆息!這嘆息聲傳遍了大地。
2. 阿爾比恩海岸一片病態的靜寂,亞美利加草地萎頓不堪!
3. 預言的影子沿著湖與河在搖曳,在大洋彼岸咕噥著。法蘭西,撕裂你的土牢吧!
4. 朝氣蓬勃的西班牙,快燒掉老羅馬的柵欄!
5. 扔掉你的鑰匙,羅馬啊!讓它掉進深淵,甚至落入永恆,
6. 並且哭泣。
7. 她❶顫抖的雙手捧著初生的哇哇大哭的恐怖。
8. 在那些無限的光明之山上,在繁星之王❷面前,站著被大西洋擋出去的新生之火!
9. 懸著灰眉白髮和雷霆般的臉,嫉妒之翅翼翻飛過海洋的上空。
10. 他的利爪在高空燃燒著;他把爪子伸進了熊熊的火焰,將那新生的奇觀拋出去,劃過星光璀燦的夜。
11. 那火,那火,在沉落!
12. 抬起頭來,抬起頭來!倫敦的公民啊,睜大你的眼睛。猶太人啊,別數金子了!回到你的石油和葡萄酒那兒去吧;阿非利加啊!黑色的阿非利加!去,有翼的思想,去加寬他的前額!
13. 火紅的四肢,燃燒的頭髮,像夕陽沉入西方的海

---

❶「永恆的女性」。

❷指上帝,在這裡代表嫉妒。

14. Wak'd from his eternal sleep, the hoary element roaring fled away:
15. Down rushd, beating his wings in vain, the jealous king; his grey brow'd councellors, thunderous warriors, curl'd veterans, among helms, and shields, and chariots, horses, elephants; banners, castles, slings and rocks,
16. Falling, rushing, ruining! buried in the ruins, on Urthona's dens;
17. All night beneath the ruins; then, their sullen flames faded, emerge round the gloomy king,
18. With thunder and fire, leading his starry hosts thro' the waste wilderness he promulgates his ten commands, glancing his beamy eyelids over the deep in dark dismay,
19. Where the son of fire in his eastern cloud, while the morning plumes her golden breast,
20. Spurning the clouds written with curses, stamps the stony law to dust, loosing the eternal horses from the dens of night, crying: 'Empire is no more! and now the lion & wolf shall cease.'

洋一樣閃射著光芒。

14. 灰色的元素從睡夢中醒來，嚎哭著逃去。

15. 徒勞地拍著翅膀的嫉妒之王❸，和他的灰眉的顧問、雷霆般的武士、鬈髮的老兵，都夾雜在頭盔、盾牌、戰車、戰馬、戰象、戰旗、投石器和石塊中間，栽了下去，

16. 倒下，栽下去，崩潰！埋進了尤索納❹窩巢上的廢墟裡。

17. 廢墟下是一片黑暗；接著，他們的慍怒的、泯滅了的火焰在那陰鬱之王❺的周圍浮現。

18. 他帶著雷電和火焰，帶著他的群星，穿過茫茫的一片荒蕪，頒布了他的十條命令❻，他閃光的眼瞼陰沉而沮喪地掃視著海洋。

19. 那裡，火的兒子❼披著東方的雲，黎明鼓起了他的金色的胸。

20. 他鄙視那用詛咒寫成的陰雲，把頑石般的律法踩入塵土之中，鬆開了夜之巢中的永恆的駿馬，喊道：「再也沒有帝國了！現在獅和狼都將絕滅。」

---

❸和前文「繁星之王」同指上帝。
❹布雷克的宗教神話體系中的神之一，象徵心靈。
❺和前文「繁星之王」、「嫉妒之王」同指上帝。
❻指十誡。
❼自由。

Chorus

Let the Priests of the Raven of dawn, no longer in deadly black, with hoarse note curse the sons of joy. Nor his accepted brethren, whom, tyrant, he calls free, lay the bound or build the roof. Nor pale religious letchery call that virginity, that wishes but acts not!

For every thing that lives is Holy.

合唱

　　不再,讓神父這黎明的渡鴉,穿著死黑的喪服,用嘶啞的調門詛咒歡樂之子;也不再,讓他公認的兄弟,他朋輩相稱的暴君,設立疆界,或建造庇蔭。也不再讓那蒼白的宗教狂熱,呼喚那可望而不可及的童貞!

　　因為每一生物皆神聖。

1793-1818

Notebook : manuscripts

筆記本・手稿詩選

William Blake, *For Children: The Gates of Paradise*, object 13, 1793

The Smile

There is a Smile of Love,
And there is a Smile of Deceit,
And there is a Smile of Smiles
In which these two Smiles meet.

And there is a Frown of Hate,
And there is a Frown of disdain,
And there is a Frown of Frowns
Which you strive to forget in vain,

For it sticks in the Heart's deep Core
And it sticks in the deep Backbone;
And no Smile that ever was smil'd,
But only one Smile alone,

That betwixt the Cradle & Grave
It only once Smil'd can be;
But, when it once is Smil'd,
There's an end to all Misery.

微笑

有一種表示愛的微笑,
也有一種虛假的微笑,
還有一種就是微笑的微笑,
其中兩種笑碰到一道。

有一種表示恨的皺眉,
也有一種輕蔑的皺眉,
還有一種就是皺眉的皺眉,
你努力去忘它也無效,

因為它扎到內心深處,
而且深深地刺進脊骨。
微笑都不會笑得永久,
卻有一種笑不在此屬──

雖然,在搖籃和墳墓之間
只能那樣地微笑一次;
可是,笑了一次之後,
所有的不幸就到了盡頭。

The Land of Dreams

'Awake, awake, my little Boy!
Thou wast thy Mother's only joy;
Why dost thou weep in thy gentle sleep?
Awake! thy Father does thee keep.'

'O, what Land is the Land of Dreams?
What are its Mountains & what are its Streams?
O Father, I saw my Mother there,
Among the Lillies by waters fair.

'Among the Lambs, clothed in white,
She walk'd with her Thomas in sweet delight.
I wept for joy, like a dove I mourn;
O! when shall I again return?'

'Dear Child, I also by pleasant Streams
Have wander'd all Night in the Land of Dreams;
But tho' calm & warm the waters wide,
I could not get to the other side.'

'Father, O Father! what do we here
In this Land of unbelief & fear?

夢國

「醒醒,醒醒,我的孩子!
你是你媽媽唯一的歡樂;
在平和的睡眠中你為何哭泣?
醒醒!爸爸一直守著你。」

「啊,夢國是怎樣的國度?
什麼樣的山,什麼樣的水?
啊,爸爸,我見到媽媽了,
在清亮的水邊的百合叢裡。」

「在羊羔中間,她穿著白衣,
帶她的湯姆怡悅地漫步,
我喜淚滿面,像鴿子般輕喚,
啊,何時我又要回去?」

「愛兒啊,我曾經到過夢國,
在怡人的水邊整夜地遊蕩;
可盡管那瀚水平靜而溫暖,
我卻不能夠到達彼岸。」

「爸爸啊,爸爸!我們為何
在這塊猜疑和恐懼的土地上?

The Land of Dreams is better far,
Above the light of the Morning Star.'

The Crystal Cabinet

The Maiden caught me in the Wild,
Where I was dancing merrily;
She put me into her cabinet
And Lock'd me up with a golden Key.

This Cabinet is formd of Gold
And Pearl & crystal shining bright,
And within it opens into a World
And a little lovely Moony Night.

Another England there I saw,
Another London with its Tower,
Another Thames & other Hills,
and another pleasant Surrey Bower.

Another Maiden like herself,
Translucent, lovely, shining clear;
Threefold each in the other closd —
O, what a pleasant trembling fear!

夢國遠遠地比這兒好啊，
它在那晨星的光芒的上方。」

水晶櫃

那少女在野地裡捉住了我，
我原在那裡歡快地跳舞；
她把我放進她的水晶櫃中，
用一把金鑰匙將我鎖住。

那櫃子是用黃金做的，
還用輝煌的水晶和珍珠，
那裡面通往一個世界，
和一個有趣可愛的月夜。

在裡面我見到另一個英國，
另一個倫敦市塔樓聳立，
另一條泰晤士河和別的山丘，
另一座薩麗宮令人神怡。

另一個像她本人的少女，
鮮艷可愛，清如冰玉，
她們倆互相三重地包孕——
多教人愉快和戰慄的恐懼！

O, what a smile! a threefold Smile
Filld me, that like a flame I burnd:
I bent to Kiss the lovely Maid,
And found a Threefold Kiss returnd.

I strove to sieze the inmost Form,
With ardor fierce & hands of flame,
But burst the Crystal Cabinet,
And like a Weeping Babe became —

A weeping Babe upon the wild,
And Weeping Woman pale reclind;
And in the outward air again
I filld with woes the passing Wind.

Auguries of Innocence

To see a World in a Grain of Sand
And a Heaven in a Wild Flower:
Hold Infinity in the palm of your hand
And Eternity in an hour.

A Robin Red breast in a Cage
Puts all Heaven in a Rage.

多甜的笑啊！三重的微笑
充滿了我，使我心熾如焚：
我彎腰親吻那可愛的少女，
得到了三倍回報的親吻。

我努力去捕捉深處的形狀，
用熾熱的感情和火熱的手，
可是那水晶櫃燒了起來，
變得像一個哭泣的嬰孩——

一個野地裡哭泣的嬰孩，
偎著個哭著的蒼白女人，
於是我又在野外，心中
充滿了悲傷這流逝的風。

天真之預言術

在一顆沙粒中見一個世界，
在一朵鮮花中見一片天空，
在你的掌心裡把握無限，
在一個鐘點裡把握無窮。

關在籠中的一隻鷗鴿
使整個天國充滿怒氣。

A dove house fill'd with doves & Pigeons
Shudders Hell thro' all its regions.
A dog starv'd at his Master's Gate
Predicts the ruin of the State.

A Horse misus'd upon the Road
Calls to Heaven for Human blood.

Each outcry of the hunted Hare
A fibre from the Brain does tear.

A Skylark wounded in the wing,
A Cherubim does cease to sing.

The Game Cock clipd & arm'd for fight
Does the Rising Sun affright.

Every Wolf's & Lion's howl
Raises from Hell a Human Soul.

The wild deer wandring here & there
Keeps the Human Soul from Care.

The Lamb misus'd breeds Public strife
And yet forgives the Butcher's Knife.

憩滿鴿子的一只鴿巢
使地獄通身戰慄震搖。
主人之門前的一條餓犬
將整個國家的毀滅預言。

路上受罪的一匹馬兒
向天國索要人類之血。

受傷的野兔的聲聲叫喚
將人類大腦的纖維撕裂。

一隻雲雀翅膀受了傷
使知識天使停止歌唱，

剪了毛準備戰鬥的鬥雞
使初升的太陽感到恐懼。

獅子和狼的每一聲吼叫
將人的靈魂從地獄勾起。

四面八方遊蕩的野鹿
使人類靈魂擺脫煩惱。

受虐的羊羔引起爭吵
然而原諒屠夫的屠刀。

The Bat that flits at close of Eve
Has left the Brain that won't Believe.

The Owl that calls upon the Night
Speaks the Unbeliever's fright.

He who shall hurt the little Wren
Shall never be belov'd by Men.

He who the Ox to wrath has mov'd
Shall never be by Woman lov'd.

The wanton Boy That kills the Fly
Shall feel the Spider's enmity.

He who torments the Chafer's sprite
Weaves a Bower in endless Night.

The Catterpiller on the Leaf
Repeats to thee thy Mother's grief.

Kill not the Moth nor Butterfly,
For the Last Judgment draweth nigh.

He who shall train the Horse to War
Shall never pass the Polar Bar.

暮色四合時掠飛的蝙蝠
已喪失不願相信的頭腦。

向黑夜祈求庇護的貓頭鷹
表明了懷疑者的恐怖驚擾。

將要殺害小鷦鷯的人
決然不會為人們所愛。

去招惹母牛發怒的人
決然不會被女人熱愛。

弄死蒼蠅的淘氣孩子
將會發覺蜘蛛的致意。

折磨金龜子小精靈的人
在不盡長夜中編織陰篷。

樹葉上的一隻小小毛蟲
使你重遭你母親的不幸。

別再捕殺毛蟲和蜻蜓，
末日的審判正在逼近。

訓練戰馬發動戰爭的人
決然逃不過雙頭棍棒。

The Begger's Dog & Widow's Cat:
Feed them & thou wilt grow fat.

the Gnat that sings his Summer's song
Poison gets from Slander's tongue.
The poison of the Snake & Newt
Is the sweat of Envy's Foot.
The Poison of the Honey Bee
Is the Artist's Jealousy.

The Prince's Robes & Beggar's Rags
Are Toadstools on the Miser's Bags.

A truth that's told with bad intent
Beats all the Lies you can invent.
It is right it should be so:
Man was made for Joy & Woe,
And when this we rightly know
Thro' the World we safely go.

Joy & Woe are woven fine,
A Clothing for the Soul divine;
Under every grief & pine
Runs a joy with silken twine.

窮人的狗和寡婦的貓，
餵牠們吧，你會長胖，

嗡嗡地唱著夏之歌的蚊蟲
帶有誹謗者舌頭上的毒水。
毒蛇以及蝾螈的毒液
是嫉妒者腳上的汗水。
毒刺長在蜜蜂的身上
正是藝術家的猜忌和提防。

乞丐的破衣和王子的絹綾
都是守財奴錢包上的黴菌。

帶著惡意道出的真言
道破你所編造的一切謊言。
事情該這樣就是這樣；
人生來就為了歡樂和悲傷，
這一點我們一旦真懂，
就能平安地穿過世上。

歡樂和悲傷編織得很妙，
正是神聖的靈魂之衣；
在種種不幸和渴望之下，
歡樂扯著線穿來穿去。

The Babe is more than swadling Bands;
Throughout all these Human Lands.
Tools were made, & Born were hands,
Every Farmer Understands.

Every Tear from Every Eye
Becomes a Babe in Eternity;
This is caught by Females bright
And return'd to its own delight.
The Bleat, the Bark, Bellow & Roar,
Are Waves that Beat on Heaven's Shore.

The Babe that weeps the Rod beneath
Writes Revenge in realms of death.

The Beggar's Rags, fluttering in Air,
Does to Rags the Heavens tear.

The Soldier, arm'd with Sword & Gun,
Palsied strikes the Summer's Sun.

The poor Man's Farthing is worth more
Than all the Gold on Afric's Shore.

One Mite wrung from the Labrer's hands
Shall buy & sell the Miser's Lands,

普天之下人類的國度裡
嬰兒比襁褓總多點什麼;
工具是造的,手是生的,
這一點連農夫也都懂得。

我們眼中的每一滴淚水,
在永恆裡變成一個嬰兒,
它被那歡快的女性捉住,
高高興興地被送了回去,
羊叫、犬吠、象吼和虎嘯
是拍擊天國之岸的波濤。

棍棒下哭泣的嬰兒
注定要在冥界還報。

空中飄揚的乞丐之衣
將天空撕得破破爛爛。

用大砲長矛武裝的兵士
將夏日的太陽打成癱瘓。

非洲海岸的全部金子,
比不上窮人半個便士。

從勞動者手中榨取的銅幣
一個就夠買守財奴的土地。

Or if protected from on high
Does that whole Nation sell & buy.

He who mocks the Infant's Faith
Shall be mock'd in Age & Death.
He who shall teach the Child to Doubt
The rotting Grave shall ne'er get out.
He who respects the Infant's faith
Triumphs over Hell & Death.

The Child's Toys & the Old Man's Reasons
Are the Fruits of the Two seasons.

The Questioner who sits so sly
Shall never know how to Reply;
He who replies to words of Doubt
Doth put the Light of Knowledge out.

The Strongest Poison ever known
Came from Caesar's Laurel Crown.

Nought can deform the Human Race
Like to the Armour's iron brace.

When Gold & Gems adorn the Plough
To peace Arts shall Envy Bow.

甚或憑藉著蒼天的保護，
夠得上買賣整片的國土。

誰要是嘲笑嬰兒的信念，
就會受歲月和死亡嘲諷。
誰要是教唆孩子去懷疑，
就會出不了腐爛的臭墳，
誰要是尊重嬰兒的信念，
就能夠戰勝地獄和死神。

孩子的遊戲和老人的理智，
乃是不同季節的不同果實。

姿態不端的質疑之人
不會懂怎樣答覆別人，
對懷疑之詞有所反應
乃是撲滅知識的光明。

古往今來最強的毒素
乃自帝王的桂冠而出。

沒有東西比鐵甲和鋼盔
更能夠使人類變成醜類。

一旦金和玉用來裝飾鐵犁，
嫉妒會下拜於和平的文藝。

A Riddle or the Cricket's Cry
Is to Doubt a fit Reply.

The Emmet's Inch & Eagle's Mile
Make Lame Philosophy to smile.

He who Doubts from what he sees
Will ne'er Believe, do what you Please.
If the Sun & Moon should doubt,
They'd immediately Go out.

To be in a Passion you Good may do,
But no Good if a Passion is in you.
The Whore & Gambler, by the State
Licenc'd build that Nation's Fate.
The Harlot's cry from Street to Street
Shall weave Old England's winding Sheet.
The Winner's Shout, the Loser's Curse,
Dance before dead England's Hearse.

Every Night & every Morn
Some to Misery are Born.
Every Morn & every Night
Some are Born to sweet delight.
Some are Born to sweet delight,

蟋蟀的鳴叫或一個謎語
是對懷疑者的合適答語。

螞蟻的一吋和鷹的一哩
使殘廢的哲理露出笑意。

誰要是懷疑目睹之物，
將一無所信永逆人意；
如果日月也產生懷疑，
那就會立刻熱盡光熄。

偶爾發怒也許有好處，
但不可心中常懷憤怒。
娼妓和賭徒要政府來批准，
反過來卻決定國家的命運。
像條條街上號叫的妓女
在為老英格蘭編織屍衣，
輸家的咒罵、贏家的高呼，
都在英格蘭的棺材前跳舞。

每一個黑夜每一個清晨
都有人為著痛苦而出生；
每一個清晨每一個黑夜
都有人生而為怡悅。
有人生而為著怡悅，

Some are Born to Endless Night.

We are led to Believe a Lie
When we see not thro' the Eye,
Which was Born in a Night, to perish in a Night,
When the Soul Slept in Beams of Light.

God Appears, & God is Light
To those poor Souls who dwell in Night,
But does a Human Form Display
To those who Dwell in Realms of day.

William Bond

I wonder whether the Girls are mad,
And I wonder whether they mean to kill,
And I wonder if William Bond will die,
For assuredly he is very ill.

He went to Church in a May morning
Attended by Fairies, one, two & three;
But the Angels of Providence drove them away,
And he return'd home in Misery.

He went not out to the Field nor Fold,

有人為著不盡長夜。

我們被帶了來相信謊言，
我們的眼睛卻一無所見——
彼生於黑暗，將終於黑暗，
而靈魂卻在光明中安眠。

上帝出現了，上帝是光明，
對住在黑暗中的可憐靈魂，
然而上帝卻顯現為人形——
對住在光明之王國的靈魂。

威廉・勃德

我很懷疑那些女孩是否瘋了，
也很懷疑她們是否在捉弄人，
我不知道威廉・勃德會不會死，
因為他的的確確病得很重呢。

他在五月裡一個早晨去教堂，
小妖精跟著，一個，兩個，三個；
但是天上的天使趕走了他們，
他在痛苦之中回到了家裡。

他不去地裡幹活也不去牧羊，

He went not out to the Village nor Town,
But he came home in a black, black cloud,
And took to his Bed & there lay down.

And an Angel of Providence at his Feet,
And an Angel of Providence at his Head,
And in the midst a Black, Black Cloud,
And in the midst the Sick Man on his Bed.

And on his Right hand was Mary Green,
And on his Left hand was his Sister Jane,
And their tears fell thro' the black, black Cloud
To drive away the sick man's pain.

'O William, if thou dost another Love,
Dost another Love better than poor Mary,
Go & take that other to be thy Wife,
And Mary Green shall her Servant be.'

'Yes, Mary, I do another Love,
Another I Love far better than thee,
And Another I will have for my Wife;
Then what have I to do with thee?'

'For thou art Melancholy, Pale,
And on thy Head is the cold Moon's shine,

他不出門去村裡也不去鎮上；
卻帶著一片黑黑的、黑黑的陰影，
回家上了床鋪，躺倒在床上。

一個天上的天使在他的腳邊，
一個天上的天使在他的頭旁，
中間是一片黑黑的、黑黑的陰影，
中間那個病人躺在床上。

他的右邊是那位瑪麗・格林，
他的左邊是他的姐姐珍妮；
灑淚滴穿黑黑的黑黑的陰影，
她們要將病人的痛苦消去。

「威廉啊，如果你是愛上了別人，
愛上了比可憐的瑪麗更好的人，
那就要那別的人做你的妻子，
瑪麗・格林我願做她的僕人。」

「是的，瑪麗，我是愛上了別人，
愛另一個遠比你好的人兒，
我要娶另一個人做我的妻；
那我何必還和你呆在一起？」

「因為你的臉色憂鬱而蒼白，
你的頭上是那清冷的月光，

But she is ruddy & bright as day,
And the sun beams dazzle from her eyne.'

Mary trembled & Mary chill'd,
And Mary fell down on the right-hand floor,
That William Bond & his Sister Jane
Scarce could recover Mary more.

When Mary woke & found her Laid
On the Right hand of her William dear —
On the Right hand of his loved Bed,
And saw her William Bond so near —

The Fairies that fled from William Bond
Danced around her Shining Head;
They danced over the Pillow white,
And the Angels of Providence left the Bed.

I thought Love livd in the hot sun shine,
But O, he loves in the Moony light!
I thought to find Love in the heat of day,
But sweet Love is the Comforter of Night.

Seek Love in the Pity of others' Woe,
In the gentle relief of another's care,
In the darkness of night & the winter's snow,

她卻像黎明一樣紅潤鮮艷,
她的眼睛閃著太陽的光芒。」

瑪麗顫抖,瑪麗直打寒顫,
瑪麗倒在床右邊的地板上,
威廉·勃德和他的姐姐珍妮,
簡直沒法使她復原和站立。

瑪麗醒來時發現自己躺著,
躺在她的親愛的威廉右邊,
躺在他的可愛的臥床之上,
她看見她的威廉就在眼前。

陪伴威廉·勃德的那些小妖精,
圍著她光輝的頭顱翩翩起舞;
她們飛舞在潔白的香枕上空,
那些天上的天使離開了床鋪。

我以為愛生活在熱烈的陽光之中,
可是啊,它是生活在月光中的!
我想在熱烈的白晝尋求到愛,
但甜蜜的愛卻是夜的安慰者。

在對他人之痛苦的同情中尋愛,
在對他人之憂愁的撫慰之中,
在夜色的幽暗和冬日的白雪之中,

In the naked & outcast, Seek Love there.

Morning

To find the Western path,
Right thro' the Gates of Wrath
I urge my way;
Sweet Mercy leads me on
With soft repentant moan:
I see the break of day.

The war of swords & spears,
Melted by dewy tears,
Exhales on high;
The Sun is freed from fears,
And with soft grateful tears
Ascends the sky.

The Birds

He. Where thou dwellest in what Grove,
    Tell me Fair one, tell me love;
    Where thou thy charming Nest dost build,
    O thou pride of every field!

在坦誠者和被棄者的中間——在那裡尋愛。

晨

為找到西去的路程
順利地通過天罰之門,
我匆匆奔跑;
和藹的仁慈引我前去,
我帶著悔恨的嘆息
見天空破曉。

戰爭的刀劍和矛弓
於露珠之淚中消融,
在高空發散;
太陽擺脫了畏懼,
掛著感激的淚滴
向天空登攀。

鳥

他:你住在哪裡,哪一片樹林,
　　告訴我,美人兒,告訴我,親親,
　　哪裡你築著迷人的香巢,
　　啊,你這普天下的驕傲!

She. Yonder stands a lonely tree,
    There I live & mourn for thee;
    Morning drinks my silent tear,
    And evening winds my sorrows bear.

He. O thou Summer's harmony,
    I have liv'd & mourn'd for thee;
    Each day I mourn along the wood,
    And night hath heard my sorrows loud.

She. Dost thou truly long for me?
    And am I thus sweet to thee?
    Sorrow now is at an End,
    O my Lover & my Friend!

He. Come on wings of joy we'll fly
    To where my Bower hangs on high;
    Come & make thy calm retreat
    Among green leaves & blossoms sweet.

Why was Cupid a Boy,
And why a boy was he?

她：那邊長著棵孤獨的樹，
　　我就住那裡，為你悲哭；
　　黎明飲乾了我無言的淚水，
　　晚風分攤著我的傷悲。

他：啊，你夏日的和諧啊，
　　我生活和悲哭都是為你：
　　每天我悲哭著沿林而行，
　　夜晚聽著我放聲哀鳴。

她：你可是真的很思慕我？
　　對於你我有那麼可愛？
　　現在悲傷已到了盡頭，
　　我的愛啊我的朋友！

他：來吧，乘著歡樂的翅膀，
　　讓我們飛向我高處的蝸居；
　　來恢復你的往日的平靜，
　　在綠葉和芬芳的鮮花叢裡。

為什麼丘比特是個男孩

為什麼丘比特是個男孩，
為何他是男而非女？

He should have been a Girl,
For ought that I can see.

For he shoots with his bow,
And the Girl shoots with her Eye,
And they both are merry & glad,
And laugh when we do cry.

And to make Cupid a Boy
Was the Cupid Girl's mocking plan;
For a boy can't interpret the thing
Till he is become a man.

And then he's so pierc'd with cares,
And wounded with arrowy smarts,
That the whole business of his life
Is to pick out the heads of the darts.

'Twas the Greeks' love of war
Turn'd Love into a Boy,
And Woman into a Statue of Stone–
And away fled every Joy.

無論如何我還是可以
認為他該是女孩。

因為他射人用弓箭，
而女孩射人用眼睛；
我們哭時，他們高興，
笑得非常之開心。

把丘比特說成是男孩，
是丘比特女孩想騙人，
因為男孩子明白事理
要等到長大成人；

那時他中了煩惱之矢，
心上受了深深的箭傷，
這就使他一生的事務
就是將箭頭拔除。

是那希臘人對戰爭的熱愛
將愛神變成了女孩，
把女性變成了石頭雕像，
使一切歡樂都逃開。

I rose up at the dawn of day–
'Get thee away, get thee away!
Prayst thou for Riches? away, away!
This is the Throne of Mammon grey.'

Said I: this sure is very odd;
I took it to be the Throne of God.
For every Thing besides I have:
It is only for Riches that I can crave.

I have Mental Joy & Mental Health,
And Mental Friends & Mental wealth;
I've a Wife I love & that loves me;
I've all But Riches Bodily.

I am in Gods pressence night & day,
And he never turns his face away;
The accuser of sins by my side does stand,
And he holds my money bag in his hand.

For my worldly things God makes him pay,
And he'd pay for more if to him I would pray;

我在晨光熹微中起身

我在晨光熹微中起身,
「你給我出去,你給我出去!
你祈求財富嗎?去,去!
這是灰色財神的寶座。」

我說:這事情真是太怪了,
我把它當成了上帝的寶座,
因為我有了其餘諸物,
若渴求我只會渴求財富。

我有精神歡樂與精神健康,
我有精神朋友與精神財富,
我有我的愛妻,她也愛我,
物質財富而外,我有了萬物。

我日夜都在上帝面前,
他從來不對我背過臉去。
罪孽的譴責者站在我旁邊,
把我的錢包攥在他手裡。

我的俗物上帝派他支付,
他會多給一些,如果我求祈;

And so you may do the worst you can do;
Be assur'd, Mr Devil, I wont pray to you.

Then If for Riches I must not Pray,
God knows, I little of Prayers need say;
So, as a Church is known by its Steeple,
If I pray it must be for other People.

He says if I do not worship him for a God,
I shall eat coarser food & go worse shod;
So, as I don't value such things as these,
You must do, Mr Devil, just as God please.

———

Never seek to tell thy love,
Love that never told can be;
For the gentle wind does move
Silently, invisibly.

I told my love, I told my love,
I told her all my heart;
Trembling cold in ghastly fears,
Ah she doth depart.

所以你可以竭盡全力去作惡,
放心吧魔鬼先生,我不想求你。

那麼,我若不必為財富而求祈,
上帝知道,我無需做什麼禱告;
所以,像教堂為它的尖頂所知,
我實是為了別人,如果我祈禱。

他說我若不把他尊崇為神,
我就得吃粗劣的食物,穿壞鞋子,
所以,既然我不重視這些東西,
魔鬼先生,你須使上帝滿意。

別試圖吐露你的愛情

別試圖吐露你的愛情——
那不能吐露的愛情;
因為那和風輕輕飄移,
默默地,不露形跡。

我吐露了愛,我吐露了愛,
我把整個心表白;
打著冷顫,萬分地恐懼——
唉!她啟步離去。

303

Soon as she was gone from me,
A traveller came by,
Silently, invisibly:
He took her with a sigh.

———

I laid me down upon a bank,
Where love lay sleeping;
I heard among the rushes dank
Weeping, Weeping.
Then I went to the heath & the wild,
To the thistles & thorns of the waste;
And they told me how they were beguil'd,
Driven out & compell'd to be chaste.

———

I saw a chapel all of gold
That none did dare to enter in,
And many weeping stood without,
Weeping, mourning, worshipping.

I saw a serpent rise between

她剛剛從我身邊離去，
就有個旅人走過；
他不言不語，不露形跡，
嘆一聲就將她俘獲。

我躺倒在一處河岸上面

我躺倒在一處河岸上面，
愛人曾安睡在那裡；
在陰濕的燈蕊草叢中，我聽見
聲聲悲泣。
於是我走向荒野的石南地，
走向野生的薊草和荊棘，
她們告訴我怎麼受了騙，
被趕出去，逼作貞女。

我看見一座全金的教堂

我看見一座全金的教堂，
誰也沒有膽量進去，
許多人悲嘆著站在外面，
悲嘆，哀哭，膜拜頂禮。

我看見一條巨蛇出現

The white pillars of the door,
And he forc'd & forc'd & forc'd
Down the golden hinges tore,

And along the pavement sweet,
Set with pearls & rubies bright,
All his slimy length he drew,
Till upon the altar white

Vomiting his poison out
On the bread & on the wine.
So I turn'd into a sty,
And laid me down among the swine.

———

I heard an Angel singing
When the day was springing:
'Mercy, Pity, Peace
Is the world's release.'

Thus he sung all day
Over the new–mown hay,
Till the sun went down,
And haycocks looked brown.

在那白色的門柱中間,
他用力擠呀擠呀擠呀,
終於擠落了黃金的鉸鏈。

沿著可愛的,鋪滿珍珠
以及燦燦寶石的通道,
他伸直他那黏滑的蛇身,
直伸到白色的祭壇上面。

他向外噴出他的毒液,
噴在麵包和啤酒上面,
於是我折進了一個豬圈,
躺在那些豬玀中間。

在黎明升起的時候

在黎明升起的時候,
我聽到一天使歌唱:
「仁慈、憐憫、和平
是這世界的解放。」

他整天這樣唱著,
在新割的乾草上方,
直到太陽西下,
乾草堆顯得昏黃。

I heard a Devil curse
Over the heath & the furze:
Mercy could be no more
If there was nobody poor

And pity no more could be
If all were as happy as we
At his curse the sun went down
And the heavens gave a frown

Down pour'd the heavy rain
Over the new reap'd grain
And Misery's increase
Is Mercy, Pity, Peace

A Cradle Song

Sleep! Sleep! beauty bright,
Dreaming o'er the joys of night;
Sleep! Sleep! in thy sleep
Little sorrows sit & weep.

Sweet Babe, in thy face
Soft desires I can trace,

我聽到個魔鬼詛咒，
在石南和荊豆的上空：
仁慈再不會存在，
如果沒有人貧窮；

「若大家一樣幸福
憐憫就不會再有。」
他咒得太陽落山，
天空皺起了眉頭。

大雨傾盆而下，
澆遍新割的莊稼，
苦難增添的乃是
和平、憐憫、仁慈。

搖籃曲

睡吧，睡吧！歡快的俊寶貝，
在夢中享盡夜間的歡愉，
睡吧，睡吧！在你的睡夢裡
很少有悲傷呆那兒哭泣。

可愛的寶貝，在你臉上
我能追覓到溫柔的情欲，

Secret joys & secret smiles,
Little pretty infant wiles.

As thy softest limbs I feel,
Smiles as of the morning steal
O'er thy cheek & o'er thy breast
Where thy little heart does rest.

O! the cunning wiles that creep
In thy little heart asleep.
When thy little heart does wake
Then the dreadful lightnings break,

From thy cheek & from thy eye,
O'er the youthful harvests nigh.
Infant wiles & infant smiles
Heaven & Earth of peace beguiles.

———

I fear'd the fury of my wind
would blight all blossoms fair & true;
And my sun it shin'd & shin'd,
And my wind it never blew.

隱秘的歡樂和隱秘的笑容,
狡猾而可愛的嬰兒的詭計。

就像我撫摸你柔軟的四肢,
黎明前,那笑容一直悄悄地
撫著你的臉,撫著你的胸,
你小小的心兒憩在胸中。

啊!你安睡著的小小心裡,
狡猾的詭計在滋蔓延伸,
一旦那小小的心兒醒來,
可怕的閃光就會裂迸——

從你的頸項和你的眼中,
照徹整個青春的收獲期,
童稚的詭計和童稚的微笑
將天國和塵世的和平騙取。

我怕我的風兒的猛烈

我怕我的風兒的猛烈
會毀了所有美而真的花朵,
我的太陽它照啊照啊,
我的風兒它從未吹過。

But a blossom fair or true
Was not found on any tree;
For all blossoms grew & grew
Fruitless, false, tho' fair to see.

———

Why should I care for the men of Thames,
Or the cheating waves of charter'd streams;
Or shrink at the little blasts of fear
That the hireling blows into my ear?

Tho' born on the cheating banks of Thames,
Tho' his waters bathed my infant limbs,
The Ohio shall wash his stains from me:
I was born a slave, but I go to be free!

———

Silent, Silent Night,
Quench the holy light
Of thy torches bright;

不過，一朵美或真的花兒
在樹上無從尋而見之，
因為一切花長啊長啊，
看上去雖美，卻華而不實。

我為什麼要介意

我為什麼要介意泰晤士河邊的人們，
介意那特轄之河的虛偽的水波？
為什麼要在小小的恐嚇之風中畏縮？
而那風是由被收買的人吹進我耳朵。

盡管出身於泰晤士河虛偽的岸邊，
盡管他的水流浴過我幼時的皮肉，
俄亥俄❶將從我身上洗去他的污點，
我生而為奴，但我在走向自由。

靜謐的，靜謐的夜

靜謐的，靜謐的夜，
熄滅你神聖的火炬，
燃著的神聖的光輝。

---

❶美國州名。

For possess'd of Day,
Thousand spirits stray
That sweet joys betray.

Why should joys be sweet
Used with deceit,
Nor with sorrows meet?

But an honest joy
Does itself destroy
For a harlot coy.

―

O lapwing thou fliest around the heath,
Nor seest the net that is spread beneath,
Why dost thou not fly among the corn fields?
They cannot spread nets where a harvest yields.

―

Thou hast a lap full of seed,

因為耽迷於白天，
無數靈魂迷失，
被甜蜜的歡樂欺騙。

為什麼歡樂慣於
因為虛假而甜蜜，
而不和痛苦相聚？

而那真正的歡愉，
卻又自我毀滅──
為一個忸怩的娼妓。

啊，田鳧

田鳧啊，你繞著荒野的石南地飛翔，
看不見在你下面撒下的網，
你為何不在小麥地裡飛行呢？
人們不能在豐熟的田地裡撒網。

你有個裝滿種子的裙兜

你有個裝滿種子的裙兜❷

---
❷英文中 lap 一字意為裙兜或山坳，這裡有雙關義。

And this is a fine country.
Why dost thou not cast thy seed,
And live in it merrily.

Shall I cast it on the sand
And turn it into fruitful land?
For on no other ground
Can I sow my seed,
Without tearing up
Some stinking weed.

The Wild Flower's Song

As I wandered the forest,
The green leaves among,
I heard a wild flower
Singing a song:

'I slept in the earth,
In the silent night,
I murmured my fears
And I felt delight.

'In the morning I went
As rosy as morn

這是個美好的邦國,
為什麼你不拋撒種子,
歡快地在其間生活?

可讓我把它們播於沙地,
把它變為富饒的土地?
因為沒別的地面
能讓我播下種子,
而無需拔掉
顯見的雜草。

野花之歌

當我漫步在森林,
在那綠葉叢裡,
我聽到一朵野花
唱著一支歌曲:

「我曾睡在大地上,
在那靜寂的夜裡,
我輕輕訴說著恐懼,
我心中感到歡喜。」

「早晨我起身離去,
像黎明一般樂觀,

To seek for new joy,
But I met with scorn.'

To Nobodaddy

Why art thou silent & invisible,
Father of Jealousy?
Why dost thou hide thyself in clouds
From every searching Eye?

Why darkness & obscurity
In all thy words & laws,
That none dare eat the fruit but from
The wily serpent's jaws?
Or is it because Secrecy gains females' loud applause?

[How to know Love from Deceit]

Love to faults is always blind
Always is to joy inclind

去尋覓新的歡愉，
但是啊，遇到了荊棘。」

致諾巴達底❸

你為何無聲而又無形，
嫉妒之父親？
你為何隱身於晦暗的陰影，
躲開尋覓的眼睛？

你的格言與律法❹，
為何都晦暗而朦朧？
使誰都不敢啃那果子，
從狡猾的毒蛇口中，
莫非神秘得到了女士們的高聲喝采？

「愛情對缺點永遠盲目」❺

愛情對缺點永遠盲目
永遠對歡樂卑躬屈膝

---

❸指上帝。

❹《聖經》中的十誡。

❺布雷克曾以此為詩題，後來刪除。

Lawless wingd & unconfind
And breaks all chains from every mind

———

Deceit to secrecy confined,
Lawful, cautious and refined,
To every thing but interest blind —
And forges fetters for the mind.

———

There souls of men are bougth and sold,
And milk-fed infancy for gold,
And youth to slaughter-houses led,
And beauty for a bit of bread.

它長著翅膀,無法無天
打碎頭腦中的一切鎖鏈

虛偽受隱秘之制約

虛偽受隱秘之制約,
拘泥、做作又謹慎;
利益而外什麼也看不到,
為人的頭腦鍛造鐐銬。

那裡在買賣人的靈魂

那裡在買賣人的靈魂,
拿吃奶的嬰兒換取金幣,
青年被帶到屠宰場裡,
美,換一點麵包而已。

Day

The Sun arises in the East,
Clothd in robes of blood & gold;
Swords & spears & wrath increas'd
All around his bosom roll'd,
Crown'd with warlike fires & raging desires.

If you trap the moment before its ripe,
The tears of repentance you'll certainly wipe;
But if once you let the ripe moment go,
You can never wipe off the tears of woe.

Eternity

He who binds to himself a joy,
Does the winged life destroy;
But he who kisses the joy as it flies,
Lives in Eternity's sunrise.

白晝

太陽從東方升起,
披著染血的黃金錦衣;
刀劍和長矛,增長的怒氣
在他的胸膛周圍滾翻,
他戴著戰火和狂烈的慾望之冠。

假如

假如在時機成熟前你把它捕捉,
你無疑將擦拭悔恨的淚水;
但假如你把成熟的時機放過,
你就擦不完悲傷的眼淚。

永恆

誰使自己受歡樂的束縛,
誰就毀掉了有翼的生命;
而誰在歡樂飛翔時吻它,
誰就將生活於永恆的黎明。

———

The look of love alarms,
Because 'tis filled with fire;
But the look of soft deceit,
Shall win the lover's hire.

Soft deceit and idleness–
These are beauty's sweetest dress.

———

My Spectre around me night & day,
Like a Wild beast guards my way;
My Emanation far within,
Weeps incessantly for my Sin.

A Fathomless & boundless deep,
There we wander there we weep;
On the hungry craving wind,
My Spectre follows thee behind.

He scents thy footsteps in the snow,

愛情的神態使人驚恐

愛情的神態使人驚恐，
因為它充滿火熱的激情；
但是溫柔的欺騙之神態，
卻會贏得情人的垂青。

溫柔的欺騙和慵懶——
是美人兒最漂亮的服裝。

我的幽靈

我的幽靈日夜將我繞，
像野獸一樣擋著我的道，
我的投影待在遠處，
為我的罪孽不停地哭。

在一個無底無邊的深淵裡，
我們傍徨，我們哭泣；
乘著那如飢似渴的風兒，
我的幽靈跟隨你。

他追蹤你留在雪地上的足跡，

Wheresoever thou dost go,
Thro the wintry hail & rain.
When wilt thou return again?

Dost thou not in Pride & scorn
Fill with tempests all my morn,
And with jealousies & fears
Fill my pleasant nights with tears?

Seven of my sweet loves thy knife
Has bereaved of their life.
Their marble tombs I built with tears,
And with cold & shuddering fears.

Seven more loves weep night & day
Round the tombs where my loves lay,
And seven more loves attend each night
Around my couch with torches bright.

And seven more Loves in my bed
Crown with wine my mournful head,
Pitying & forgiving all
Thy transgressions great & small.

你走到哪裡他跟到哪裡,
穿過冬日的冰雹和雨,
什麼時候你才回去?❺

你是否以輕蔑和驕矜
把風暴裝滿我的黎明,
是否懷著嫉妒和恐懼
把淚水裝滿我歡樂的夜裡?

我的七個甜蜜的愛人,
已在你的刀下喪生,
他們的玉石墓,是我用淚、
用冰冷的發抖的恐懼造成。

另七個愛人日夜流淚,
躺在我愛人的墳墓周圍,
另七個舉著輝煌的火炬,
每夜都來圍著我的睡椅。

另七個愛人上我的床鋪,
用美酒裝飾我的頭顱,
她們可憐並且原諒,
你的所有大小罪狀。

---

❺以下是「投影」和「我」的對話。

When wilt thou return & view
My loves & them to life renew?
When wilt thou return & live?
When wilt thou pity as I forgive?

O'er my sins thou sit and moan:
Hast thou no sins of thy own?
O'er my sins thou sit and weep,
And lull thy own sins fast asleep.

What transgressions I commit
Are for thy transgressions fit.
They thy harlots, thou their slave;
And my bed becomes their grave.

Never, Never, I return:
Still for Victory I burn.
Living thee alone Ill have;
And when dead Ill be thy Grave.

Thro the Heavn & Earth & Hell,
Thou shaelt never never quell;
I will fly & thou pursue,
Night & Morn the flight renew.

poor, pale, pitiable form

你何時回來看我的愛人，
並且使她們獲得新生？
你何時才會回來居住？
你何時原諒，我既已寬恕？

你坐在我的罪孽上悲哭，
你自己是否有過失之處？
你坐在我的罪孽上流淚，
催你自己的罪快快入睡。

我所承認的所有過錯
對你來說最合適不過，
她們是娼妓，你是奴隸；
我的床變成了她們的墓地。

不、不、我絕不回去：
我依然在為勝利而燃燒。
活著，我要讓你孤獨，
死了，我來做你的墳墓。

穿過天國、人間和地獄，
你可以永遠，永遠得寧息；
我要飛翔，你要追隨，
日日夜夜飛了又飛。

在暴風雨之中，我的容顏

That I follow in a storm;
Iron tears and groans of lead
Bind around my aching head.

Till I turn from Female Love
And root up the Infernal Grove,
I shall never worthy be
To Step into Eternity.

And to end thy cruel mocks,
Annihilate thee on the rocks,
And another form create
To be subservient to my Fate.

Let us agree to give up Love,
And root up the infernal Grove;
Then shall we return & see
The worlds of happy Eternity.

& Throughout all Eternity
I forgive you, you forgive me.
As our dear Redeemer said:
This the Wine & this the Bread.

多麼蒼白多麼可憐；
鉛的嘆息和鐵的淚珠
絪住我的疼痛的頭顱。

等我擺脫了女性的愛情
並且脫離了地獄的叢林
我才能擁有資格與緣份
邁步進入不朽的永恆

並且把你消滅在岩石上
結束你那殘忍的嘲笑
並且創造出另一個形象
由我的命運來主宰和主導

讓我們同意放棄愛情
並且脫離地獄的業林
那時我們就會回去
看見幸福的永恆之境地

通過整個的永恆之國
我原諒了你，你原諒了我
正如那親愛的拯救者所道
這個是酒，這個是麵包

Selected Poems of William Blake

I saw a monk of Charlemaine
Arise before my sight;
I talked with the grey monk where he stood
In beams of infernal light.

Gibbon arose with a lash of steel,
And Voltaire with a racking wheel:
The Schools, in clouds of learning rolled,
Arose with war in iron and gold.

'Thou lazy monk,' they sound afar,
'In vain condemning glorious war!
And in thy cell thou shalt ever dwell.
Rise, War, and bind him in his cell!'

The blood red ran from the grey monk's side,
His hands and feet were wounded wide,
His body bent, his arms and knees
Like to the roots of ancient trees.

查理曼的修士

我見到一個查理曼的修士
浮現在我的視野裡，
我與這灰衣修士❻交談，
他站在地獄的光線裡。

吉本出現，帶著鋼鞭，
伏爾泰帶著個破輪露面：
那學院❼，在學術的陰雲中翻滾，
伴著那披金戴鐵的戰爭。

他們在遠處：「你這懶修士，
譴責戰爭是枉費口舌！
你將永遠住在陋室裡，
來，戰爭，把他綑起！」

修士身上流下了鮮血，
他的手和腳受了重傷，
他弓著身體、雙膝和臂膀
就像古老的樹根一樣。

---

❻聖方濟會(Franciscan)教士，常著灰衣。
❼法蘭西學院。

'I see, I see,' the mother said,
'My children will die for lack of bread.
What more has the merciless tyrant said?'
The monk sat down on her stony bed.

His eye was dry, no tear could flow;
A hollow groan first spoke his woe.
He trembled and shuddered upon the bed;
At length with a feeble cry he said:

When God commanded this hand to write
In the studious hours of deep midnight,
He told me that all I wrote should prove
The bane of all that on earth I love.

My brother starved between two walls,
His children's cry my soul appals;
I mocked at the rack and griding chain,
My bent body mocks at their torturing pain.

Thy father drew his sword in the north,
With his thousands strong he is marched forth;
Thy brother has armed himself in steel
To revenge the wrongs thy children feel.

But vain the sword and vain the bow,

「我懂了,我懂了,」母親說道,
「我的孩子將飢饉而亡,
那不仁的暴君還能怎樣?」
修士坐在她冰硬的床上。

他眼睛枯澀,淚已哭乾,
一聲長嘆道破了悲傷。
他在床上瑟瑟地抖顫,
最後無力地開始哭講:

在勤學的深夜,當這雙手
受命於上帝而寫作的時候,
他說我寫下的一切將證明
塵世間我所愛的一切的毒性。

我兄弟求生無門而餓死,
你的孩子們哭得我心悸;
我嘲笑哪嘎嘎響的破舊鎖鏈,
我傴僂的身體嘲笑酷刑的熬煎。

你父親在北方拔出利劍,
率萬千壯士奮勇向前;
你兄弟舉鋼叉拚殺廝鬥
在為你孩子們的遭遇復仇。

但利劍和弓矢無濟於我們,

They never can work war's overthrow.
The hermit's prayer and the widow's tear
Alone can free the world from fear.

The hand of vengeance sought the bed
To which the purple tyrant fled;
The iron hand crushed the tyrant's head,
And became a tyrant in his stead.

Until the tyrant himself relent,
The tyrant who first the black bow bent,
Slaughter shall heap the bloody plain;
Resistance and war is the tyrant's gain.

But the tear of love and forgiveness sweet,
And submission to death beneath his feet–
The tear shall melt the sword of steel,
And every wound it has made shall heal.

A tear is an intellectual thing,
And a sigh is the sword of an angel king,
And the bitter groan of the martyr's woe
Is an arrow from the Almighty's bow.

它們永不能打倒戰爭。
唯隱士的新居和寡婦的哭泣
才能使這世界擺脫恐懼。

復仇的手在那床上搜
穿紫袍的暴君聞聲逃走,
鐵手捏碎了暴君的頭頸,
又取而代之成了暴君。

拉彎第一張黑弓的暴君,
如果他自己不發善心,
屠殺將堆屍於血染的原野上;
暴君的所求乃戰爭與抵抗。

唯有愛之淚——甜美的寬恕
和死神腳下的順從的屈服——
唯有它能融化鋼鐵的利劍,
使每一處劍傷痊癒和復原。

因為眼淚帶有智性,
嘆息是那天使的利劍,
不幸的殉難者悲苦的呻吟
是全能者之弓發出的飛箭。

Mock on, Mock on, Voltaire, Rousseau;
Mock on, Mock on; 'tis all in vain
You throw the sand against the wind,
And the wind blows it back again

And every sand becomes a Gem
Reflected in the beams divine
Blown back they blind the mocking Eye,
But Still in Israel's paths they shine.

The Asoms of Democritus,
And Nenton's Particles of light
And sands upon the Red sea shore,
Where Israel's tents do shine do shine so bright.

You don't believe– I won't attempt to make ye.
You are asleep– I won't attempt to wake ye.
Sleep on! sleep on! while in your pleasant dreams
Of reason you may drink of life's clear streams.

嘲笑吧，嘲笑吧，伏爾泰、盧梭

嘲笑吧，嘲笑吧，伏爾泰、盧梭；
嘲笑吧，嘲笑吧，這是枉費心機！
你們迎風揚起了沙子，
風又把它們打了回去。

每顆沙子都變成玉石，
熠熠地映射著神聖的光芒；
打回去打瞎了嘲笑的眼睛，
依然在以色列的路上放光。

德謨克利特的原子，
牛頓的光的粒子，
都是紅海岸邊的沙子，
那裡以色列的篷帳輝煌無比。

你不信

你不信──我不想使你相信。
你睡著──我不想把你喚醒。
睡吧！睡吧！在理性的美夢裡，
你也許會將生命的清流飲取。

Reason and Newton, they are quite two things,
For so the swallow and the sparrow sings.

Reason says 'Miracle,' Newton says 'Doubt.'
Aye, that's the way to make all Nature out:
'Doubt, doubt and don't believe without experiment!'
That is the very thing that Jesus meant,
When he said 'Only believe! believe and try!
Try, try and never mind the reason why!'

———

'Now Art has lost its mental Charms,
France shall subdue the World in Arms.'
So spoke an Angel at my birth;
Then said 'Descend thou upon Earth,
Renew the Arts on Britain's Shore,
And France shall fall down & adore.
With works of Art their Armies meet
And War shall sink beneath thy feet.
But if thy Nation Arts refuse,
And if they scorn the immortal Muse,
France shall the arts of Peace restore
And save thee from the Ungrateful shore.'
Spirit who lov'st Britannia's Isle
Round which the fiends of Commerce smile ——
  Cetera desunt

燕子和麻雀唱的是不同的歌曲，
理性和牛頓，也迥然相異。

理性說「奇蹟」，牛頓說「懷疑」──
唉！那就是理解整個自然的方式：
「懷疑，懷疑，沒經驗過的就別信！」
而那正是耶穌所指的事情，
他說：「唯有相信！相信和嘗試！
嘗試！嘗試！別介意有何道理！」

藝術已失去了內在的魅力

藝術已失去了內在的魅力，
法蘭西將對世界訴諸武力。
我出生時一位天使對我講：
把你降生到這個世界之上，
在不列顛的海岸復興藝術，
法國將倒下並膜拜和匍匐；
他們的武器將遇你的作品，
戰爭在你腳下將衰微一盡；
如果汝國對藝術加以拒絕，
對那不朽的繆斯報以輕蔑，
法國就將恢復和平的藝術，
從那粗野的海岸把你救出。

The Golden Net

Three Virgins at the break of day:
'Whither, young Man, whither away
Alas for woe! alas for woe!'
They cry, & tears for ever flow.
The one was Cloth'd in flames of fire,
The other Cloth'd in iron wire,
The other Cloth'd in tears & signs
Dazling bright before my Eyes.
They bore a Net of golden twine
To hang upon the Branches fine.
Pitying I wept to see the woe
That Love & Beauty undergo,
To be consum'd in burning Fires
And in ungratified desires,
And in tears cloth'd Night & day
Melted all my Soul away.
When they saw my Tears, a Smile
That did Heaven itself beguile,
Bore the Golden Net aloft
As on downy Pinions soft,
Over the Morning of my day.
Underneath the Net I stray,

金網

天光破曉處有三位處女——
「枯萎了,年輕人,你已萎去?
多麼傷心!多麼傷心!」
她們哭著,淚流個不停。
一位處女穿的是火焰,
另一位處女穿的是鐵絲,
第三位穿的是淚水和嘆息,
輝煌奪目地在我面前。
她們揹來一張金絲網,
把它掛在漂亮的樹枝上。
看著愛與美經受苦難,
我滿懷同情,不勝悲嘆;
看著她們在熊熊的火焰
和永不滿足的慾望裡枯萎,
我的整個靈魂消融,
化入了日夜流淌的眼淚;
當我的淚水被她們看到,
一個上帝哄自己的微笑,
高高掛在那張金網上,
像懸起輕柔的羽毛一樣,
罩住了我的黎明時刻。
我在金網之下消失了,

Now entreating Burning Fire
Now entreating Iron Wire,
Now intreating Tears & Sighs—
O! when will the morning rise ?

The Mental Traveller

I travell'd thro' a Land of Men,
A Land of Men & Women too;
And heard & saw such dreadful things
As cold Earth wanderers never knew.

For there the Babe is born in joy
That was begotten in dire woe;
Just as we Reap in joy the fruit
Which we in bitter tears did sow.

And if the Babe is born a Boy
He's given to a Woman Old,
Who nails him down upon a rock,
Catches his shrieks in cups of gold.

She binds iron thorns around his head,
She pierces both his hands & feet,
She cuts his heart out at his side,

此時我求教於熊熊烈火,
此時我求教於鐵絲,
此時我求教於眼淚和嘆息——
啊!黎明將在何時重現?

內心旅行者

我途經一個男人的國度,
這國度有男人也有女人;
我所見聞的駭人的事情,
乃冷漠的塵世旅行者所未聞。

那裡的嬰兒出生於歡樂,
然而受孕於不幸的傷悲;
正如我們歡樂地收割,
播種時卻灑下悲酸之淚。

如果那嬰兒生而為男,
他就被交給一個老婦,
她將他釘在石頭上面,
用金杯接他那尖聲的嚎哭。

她用鐵蒺藜綁住他的頭,
她刺穿他的腳也刺穿他的手,
她割下他的心放在旁邊,

To make it feel both cold & heat.

Her fingers number every Nerve,
Just as a Miser counts his gold;
She lives upon his shrieks & cries,
And she grows young as he grows old.

Till he becomes a bleeding youth,
And she becomes a Virgin bright;
Then he rends up his Manacles,
And binds her down for his delight.

He plants himself in all her Nerves,
Just as a Husbandman his mould;
And she becomes his dwelling place
And Garden fruitful seventy fold.

An aged Shadow, soon he fades,
Wandring round an Earthly Cot,
Full filled all with gems & gold
Which he by industry had got.

And these are the gems of the Human Soul,
The rubies & pearls of a love–sick eye,
The countless gold of the aching heart,
The martyr's groan & the lover's sigh.

讓它對熱與冷都有所體驗。

她的手把每根神經都數過，
就像吝嗇鬼查點其黃金；
她靠他的哭嚎生活，
他愈益年長，她愈益年輕。

最後他變成個流血的青年，
她則變成了鮮艷的處女，
然後他將他的手銬砸爛，
為了取樂將她綑起。

他用她全部的神經來育己，
像丈夫種他的模型一般；
她變成了他的居住之地
和一個七十倍豐產的果園。

他很快衰老成老年的影子，
繞著塵世的小屋踱步，
他身上裝滿黃金和寶石
那是他勤勞所致的財富。

這是人類靈魂的寶石，
是相思的眼睛裡的珍珠和紅玉，
是痛苦的心靈中的無數金子，
是殉難者的呻吟和情人的嘆息。

They are his meat, they are his drink;
He feeds the Beggar & the Poor
And the wayfaring Traveller:
For ever open is his door.

His grief is their eternal joy;
They make the roofs & walls to ring;
Till from the fire on the hearth
A little Female Babe does spring.

And she is all of solid fire
And gems & gold, that none his hand
Dares stretch to touch her Baby form,
Or wrap her in his swaddling-band.

But She comes to the Man she loves,
If young or old, or rich or poor;
They soon drive out the aged Host,
A Beggar at another's door.

He wanders weeping far away,
Until some other take him in;
Oft blind & age-bent, sore distrest,
Untill he can a Maiden win.

這是他的食物和飲料；
他以此款待窮人乞丐
以及徒步旅行的旅人：
他的門永遠對他們敞開。

他的苦是他們永恆的歡樂；
他們使屋頂和牆壁唱歌；
直到荒原上的野火之中
誕生了一個女性的嬰兒。

她是全部固體的火焰、
寶石和黃金，嬰兒的身體
他不敢伸手撫摸，也不敢
用他的襁褓把她裹起。

但她尋找她所愛的人們了，
不管窮或富，青年或老年；
年老的主人立刻被逐，
行乞於他人的大門之前。

他流著淚漂泊，走向遠方，
最後他被人收留供養，
他又老又駝、渾身痛、眼睛瞎，
最後他贏得了一位姑娘。

And to allay his freezing Age,
The Poor Man takes her in his arms;
The Cottage fades before his sight,
The Garden & its lovely Charms.

The Guests are scatter'd thro' the land,
For the Eye altering alters all;
The Senses roll themselves in fear,
And the flat Earth becomes a Ball.

The Stars, Sun, Moon, all shrink away:
A desert vast without a bound,
And nothing left to eat or drink,
And a dark desert all around.

The honey of her Infant lips,
The bread & wine of her sweet smile,
The wild game of her roving Eye,
Does him to Infancy beguile.

For as he eats & drinks he grows
Younger & younger every day;
And on the desert wild they both
Wander in terror & dismay.

Like the wild Stag she flees away,

為了減輕他凍僵的年紀,
這可憐人把她抱在懷裡;
小屋在他面前漸漸凋敝,
花園也失去了可愛的魅力。

變化的景色改變了一切,
於是旅客遍布於九州;
感官恐懼地到處亂滾,
平坦的大地變成了圓球。

日月星辰,全部消隱:
荒原茫茫,天邊也無沿,
沒有食物,也沒有水,
四周全是茫茫的荒原。

她的微笑裡的酒和麵包,
她的稚嫩雙唇上的甘蜜,
她流盼的眼睛裡任性的遊戲,
將他哄向嬰兒時期。

因為他每天又吃又喝,
所以他變得愈益年輕,
在荒野上面,他們兩個
恐懼而沮喪地四處飄零。

她像野鹿一樣地逃走,

Her fear plants many a thicket wild;
While he pursues her night & day,
By various arts of Love beguil'd,

By various arts of Love & Hate,
Till the wide desert planted o'er
With Labyrinths of wayward Love,
Where roam the Lion, Wolf & Boar.

Till he becomes a wayward Babe,
And she a weeping woman Old.
Then many a Lover wanders here;
The Sun & Stars are nearer roll'd.

The trees bring forth sweet Ectasy
To all who in the desert roam;
Till many a City there is Built,
And many a pleasant Shepherd's home.

But when they find the frowning Babe,
Terror strikes thro' the region wide:
They cry 'The Babe! the Babe is Born!'
And flee away on Every side.
For who dare touch the frowning form,
His arm is wither'd to its root;
Lions, Boars, Wolves, all howling flee,

用恐懼種下許多野灌木叢;
他追趕著她,日夜不休,
被各種愛情的藝術所誆哄,

他受騙於各種愛與恨的藝術,
終於,在廣闊的荒野上面
布滿了任性的愛情的迷宮,
野豬、獅和狼漫遊其間。

終於,她變成了哭泣的老婦,
他則變成了任性的嬰兒。
太陽和星辰更近地運轉著,
許多的情人漫遊到這兒。

樹上結出了甜蜜的狂喜
奉給荒野的每一位遊客;
終於建起了許多城市,
許多牧人的快樂的家舍。

可他們發現了那皺眉的嬰兒,
整個地區為恐怖所籠罩——
他們喊著「那個嬰兒!嬰兒出生了!」
他們逃了,連滾帶跑。
因為誰敢摸那皺眉的形象,
手臂就會枯萎無遺;
野豬和獅狼齊吼著奔逃,

And every Tree does shed its fruit.

And none can touch that frowning form,
Except it be a Woman Old;
She nails him down upon the Rock,
And all is done as I have told.

Great things are done when Men & Mountains meet,
This is not done by Jostling in the Steet.

To God

If you have formed a Circle to go into,
Go into it yourself & see how you would do.

Terror in the house does roar,
But Pity stands bfore the door.

每棵樹木都凋落了果實。

除非那人是一個老婦，
沒人敢摸那皺眉的形象；
她把他釘在石頭上面，
就像我前面説過的那樣。

偉大的事業

偉大的事業建樹於人與群山相會的時候，
這是大街上的擁擠所不能造就。

致上帝

如果你造了圈套叫人去鑽，
你先鑽進去，看看你會怎麼辦。

恐怖與慈悲

恐怖在屋裡怒吼，
慈悲卻站在門口。

And did those feet in ancient time,
Walk upon Englands mountains green?
And was the holy Lamb of God,
On Englands pleasant pastures seen?

And did the Countenance Divine,
Shine forth upon our clouded hills?
And was Jerusalem builded here,
Among these dark Satanic Mills?

Bring me my Bow of burning gold!
Bring me my Arrows of desire!
Bring me my Spear! O clouds unfold!
Bring me my Chariot of fire!

I will not cease from Mental Fight,
Nor shall my Sword sleep in my hand,
Till we have built Jerusalem,
In England's green & pleasant Land.

要是遠古時那些聖足……❽

要是遠古時那些聖足，
曾在英格蘭的群山上徜徉？
要是那神聖的上帝的羊羔，
到過英格蘭的快樂的牧場？

那張神聖的臉龐，
可曾照亮我們陰雲中的山巒？
耶路撒冷可曾建起，
在這些昏暗的撒旦的磨坊❾之間？

把我那灼亮的金弓帶給我，
把我那願望的箭矢帶給我，
帶給我長矛！招展的雲彩呀！
把我那烈火的戰車帶給我！

我不會停止內心的戰鬥，
我的劍也不會在手中安眠，
直到我們建立起耶路撒冷，
在英格蘭青翠而快樂的地面。

---

❽此詩亦出現在布雷克長詩《彌爾頓》(Milton)的導言。
❾雙關義，原文mill也指工廠。

布雷克年表
（雕刻繪畫生涯從簡）

1757	11月28日威廉・布雷克 (William Blake) 誕生於倫敦布羅德 (Broad) 大街28號。
1761	幻覺見到上帝，後又見田野裡一大樹上棲滿天使。
1768	在家中受初步教育後，被送入亨利・巴斯的繪畫學校學習至1772年。
1769	開始創作抒情詩，後收入《詩的素描》(*Poetical Sketches*)。
1772	開始長達七年之久的雕刻藝徒生涯。次年作成最早的一幅名作《阿里瑪西的約瑟夫》。
1779	進入皇家學院學藝。
1780	繪成《快樂的一天》初稿，首展於皇家學院。在曼德威河流域搜集素材時與同行之藝術家一同被誤認為法國間諜而被捕入獄。
1782	娶文盲凱瑟琳・布歇爾(Catherine Boucher, 1762-1831)為妻，居倫敦格林(Green)大街23號，後又遷至布羅德大街28號。教凱瑟琳讀書寫字和製版畫。布雷克夫婦相伴終生，無嗣。
1783	《詩的素描》付梓，但未外售。在沙龍裡吟唱自己的詩，這種活動持續了一生。
1784	在布羅德大街27號經營印刷店。創作《月中島》(*An Island in the Moon*)，包括《天真之歌》(*Songs of Innocence*)最初的一些詩，但未出版。
1785	印刷店破產，移居波蘭街。

布雷克年表

1787　幼弟羅伯特早逝。威廉・布雷克看見他的靈魂穿過屋頂冉冉上升，鼓掌樂之。

1788　參加斯威頓伯格 (Swedenborg) 協會，創作《先知書》(Illuminated Books) 中最早的繪圖作品《一切宗教歸一》(All Religions Are One) 和《無自然宗教》(There Is No Natural Religion)。

1789　創作《特里爾》(Tirel，未出版)，出版《天眞之歌》和《塞爾書》(The Book of Thel)。

1790　開始創作《天國與地獄的婚姻》(The Marriage of Heaven and Hell)。移居泰晤士河對岸的 Lambeth 區 Hercules 大樓 13 號。

1791　《法國大革命》(The French Revolution) 付梓，但未發行。

1792　3月，完成《天國與地獄的婚姻》。

1793　在筆記中寫道：「我活不了五年了，能活一年便是奇跡。」出版《阿爾比恩女兒們的幻象》(Visions of the Daughters of Albion)，《給孩子們：樂園之門》(For Children: The Gates of Paradise) 和《美利堅：一個預言》(America: A Prophecy)。

1794　出版《天眞與經驗之歌》(Songs of Innocence and of Experience)、《歐羅巴：一個預言》(Europe: A Prophecy) 和《尤利壬書之一》(The First Book of Urizen)。

1795　出版《羅斯之歌》(The Song of Los)、《羅斯書》(The Book of Los) 和《阿罕尼亞書》(The Book *of Ahania*)。9月受到「騷擾和搶劫」。

1797　修改費時十年的《四天神》(*The Four Zoas*)，不幸手稿遺失。

1800-1803　移居費芬 (Felpham)，在詩人威廉・海萊 (William Hayley) 的資助下生活。手稿詩作也許作於此時。白天執行海萊的藝術計劃，晚間重寫《四天神》。學習希臘文、拉丁文和希伯來文。

1803　8月12日把一名醉酒的士兵逐出花園，因而被控挑起暴動，威脅國王。9月返倫敦，居爾頓南 (South Moton) 街17號。

1804　1月11日至12日契切斯特 (Chichester) 法庭在聽審者的歡呼聲中宣布布雷克無罪。

1807　筆記中寫道：「1807年1月20日，星期二，夜間兩點至晨七點——絕望。」5月，皇家學院展出菲利普 (Phillip) 所作布雷克像。

1810　筆記中寫道：「1810年5月23日發現金字。」

1818　在筆記本上寫就《永久的福音》(*The Everlasting Gospel*)將《樂園之門》改為《致男女們》(*To the Sexes*)。

1820　出版《耶路撒冷》(*Jerusalem*) 卷一、《拉奧孔》(*The Laocoon*)、《評荷馬的詩》(*On Homer's Poetry*) 和《論維吉爾》(*On Virgil*)。

1821　出售畫作維生。移居斯特蘭德 (Strand) 大街芳亭 (Fountain) 大院3號。

1827　8月12日早晨八時去世，享年六十九歲。臨終時吟唱著在天國所見的景物。

好站拾穗

一、布雷克詩文搶先看

- **Project Gutenberg**
  古騰堡計劃。Michael Hart 自 1971 年開始將公共版權圖書數位化，目前有兩萬本書可免費下載，並且持續更新增加中。
  http://www.gutenberg.org

- **The Oxford Text Archive**
  牛津全文檔案室。Lou Burnard 於 1976 年開始收集、校訂、建立可靠的資料庫，推廣電子全文在學術社群中的使用。
  http://ota.ahds.ac.uk

二、布雷克簡介＆圖像創作

- **Wikimedia: William Blake**
  維基百科英文版。提供布雷克生平與作品簡析、圖像共享與連結。
  http://en.wikipedia.org/wiki/William_Blake
  http://commons.wikimedia.org/wiki/William_Blake

- **San Francisco Blue Neon Alley: William Blake**
  「敲打的一代」(Beat Generation)作家與文學主題網站下建置的布雷克網頁。提供布雷克詩選、簡介與圖像連結、搜尋引擎。
  http://www.neonalley.org/blake.html

- **Artcyclopedia: William Blake**
  在線上藝術百科搜尋布雷克。可連結至世界各國博物館、美術館、私人畫廊與線上資料庫,瀏覽布雷克的圖像創作。
  http://www.artcyclopedia.com/artists/blake_william.html

- **Tyger of Wrath: William Blake in the National Gallery of Victoria**
  澳洲維多利亞國家美術館(National Gallery of Victoria)收藏176幅布雷克的水彩畫與銅版蝕刻作品,為當代重要的布雷克典藏之一。
  http://www.ngv.vic.gov.au/blake

- **The William Blake Page**
  藝術家Gail Gastfield和工程師Richard Record建置的布雷克網頁。完整呈現《天真與經驗之歌》彩色圖文版,並可一窺《約伯記》、《天國與地獄的婚姻》等書的圖像創作。
  http://www.gailgastfield.com/Blake.html

- **Jerusalem**
  布雷克晚年的詩畫鉅作《耶路撒冷》(*Jerusalem: The Emanation of the Giant Albion*)的超媒體網頁。由美國北卡羅萊納大學教堂山分校(University of North Carolina at Chapel Hill)英語系Joseph Viscomi教授指導研究生製作,須先申請才能瀏覽。
  http://sites.unc.edu/blake/jerusalem.html

三、布雷克研究&教學

- **The William Blake Archive**
  布雷克檔案室。目前最詳盡、精美、好用的布雷克線上資

料庫,各方強力推薦!由美國國會圖書館(Library of Congress)贊助,蓋堤助成金基金會(Getty Grant Program)、維吉尼亞大學人文學科進階科技中心(The Institute for Advanced Technology in the Humanities, University of Virginia)共同建構,可用關鍵字搜尋圖像與全文,比較不同版本的布雷克圖像創作。2003年獲MLA傑出學術版本獎(MLA Prize for a Distinguished Scholarly Edition, 2003)。
http://www.blakearchive.org

- **Blake Digital Text Project**
布雷克數位文本計劃。美國喬治亞大學(University of Georgia)英語系Nelson Hilton教授主持,提供資深布雷克研究者David V. Erdman編輯的《威廉布雷克詩文全集》(*The Complete Poetry and Prose of William Blake*)電子全文與《天真與經驗之歌》版畫的單色影像,可局部放大,附現代譯文與解析。
http://www.english.uga.edu/nhilton

- **Blake: An Illustrated Quarterly**
布雷克專題季刊。1967年創刊於美國加州大學柏克萊分校,由該校資深布雷克研究者Morton D. Paley教授與紐約羅徹斯特大學(University of Rochester)英語系Morris Eaves教授主編。
http://www.rochester.edu/college/eng/blake

- **The Rossetti Archive: The Complete Writings and Pictures**
羅塞蒂檔案室。英國詩人、前拉斐爾派(Pre-Raphaelites)畫家羅塞蒂(Dante Gabriel Rossetti,1828-1882)曾收藏布雷克的筆記本,並謄寫、編輯他的詩作,因此該筆記本又稱「羅塞蒂手稿」(The Rossetti Manuscript)。本站為羅塞蒂主題

研究網站，提供完整且經考證的羅塞蒂手稿、畫作與出版品資料。本站為十九世紀電子學術網絡架構(Networked Infrastructure for Nineteenth-century Electronic Scholarship)下的子計劃。
http://www.rossettiarchive.org

- **The Blake Society**
  英國布雷克協會。1985年創立於布雷克受洗的倫敦聖詹姆士大教堂（St. James Church, Piccadilly, London），致力於引介與推廣布雷克的創作。每年出版《布雷克學報》(*The Blake Journal*)，是研究布雷克的重要材料。2007年籌辦一系列紀念布雷克誕生250週年的活動。
  http://www.blakesociety.org.uk

- **The Blake Multimedia Project**
  布雷克多媒體教學計劃。美國加州州立科技大學(California Polytechnic State University San Luis Obispo)英語系教授Steven Marx製作，可下載《約伯記》、《天眞與經驗之歌》、《天國與地獄的婚姻》的hypertext版本，提供術語解釋、評析與討論議題。
  http://cla.calpoly.edu/~smarx/Blake/blakeproject

四、浪漫時期研究

- **Romanticism on the Net**
  以英國浪漫時期研究為主題的國際學術期刊(ISSN:1467-1255)。由任教於加拿大蒙特婁大學(Université de Montréal)英語系，專精十九世紀與浪漫時期英國文學的Michael Eberle-Sinatra教授主編，提供線上閱讀與研討會訊息。
  http://www.ron.umontreal.ca

- **William Blake and Visual Culture: a Special Issue of *ImageTexT***
  視覺文化線上期刊 *ImageTexT* (ISSN: 1549-6732)。美國佛羅里達大學英語系出版。2007年2月的「布雷克與視覺文化」特輯(Vol 3 No.2)，收錄多篇探討布雷克圖像創作的專題論文。
  http://www.english.ufl.edu/imagetext/archives/v3_2

- **Romantic Circles**
  以浪漫時期文學與文化研究為主題的學術網站。美國馬里蘭大學英語系與人文學科科技中心(The Maryland Institute for Technology in the Humanities) Neil Fraistat教授、芝加哥大學英語系Steven E. Jones教授與加州大學聖塔芭芭拉分校英語系Carl Stahmer教授共同主持，獲選為美國國家人文基金會(National Endowment for the Humanities, NEH)優良網站。2006年建置的「詩人論詩人」(Poets on Poets)聲音資料庫尤其獲得詩歌基金會(The Poetry Foundation)的推薦與好評。
  http://www.rc.umd.edu

- **The North American Society for the Study of Romanticism**
  北美浪漫時期研究學會。創立於加拿大西安大略大學(The University of Western Ontario)，每年《歐洲浪漫時期評論》(*European Romantic Review*)春季號為該學會論文特輯。由此可連結許多以浪漫時期文學、美術與音樂等跨領域研究為主題的美加學會網站。
  http://publish.uwo.ca/~nassr

- **British Association for Romantic Studies (BARS)**
  英國浪漫時期研究協會。協助並推廣浪漫時期的文化史研

究,電子報與會刊上提供書訊、書評、各地研討會與獎助訊息。
http://www.bars.ac.uk

- **Voice of the Shuttle: Romantics**
探討十八至十九世紀浪漫時期文藝的線上資料庫。加州大學聖塔芭芭拉分校英語系Alan Liu教授主持,提供期刊論文、專題計劃、課程簡介、研討會訊息等豐富的學術資源。
http://vos.ucsb.edu/browse.asp?id=2750

- **Romantic Chronology**
浪漫時期編年史。邁阿密大學英語系Laura Mandell教授和加州大學聖塔芭芭拉分校英語系Alan Liu教授主持建構。以年代、主題與關鍵字檢索浪漫時期研究文獻與網頁。
http://www.english.ucsb.edu:591/rchrono

- **The Bluestocking Archive**
藍襪子檔案室。由專精浪漫時期研究的麻薩諸塞大學(University of Massachusetts Boston)英語系Elizabeth Fay教授主持。十八世紀中期,英國社會運動者Elizabeth Montagu打破社會陳規,組織女性文藝沙龍。由於部份與會者家貧穿不起黑絲襪,只好穿藍色的絨線襪,便自稱藍襪社(Blue Stocking Society);「藍襪子」因此成為後世女性知青的代稱。本網站提供此社群與英國浪漫主義極盛時期的研究文獻。
http://www.faculty.umb.edu/elizabeth_fay/toc2.htm

五、布雷克&詩迷俱樂部

- **British Library Online Gallery: William Blake's Notebook**

大英圖書館線上展覽館。用 Turning the Pages 影像瀏覽軟體，布雷克的筆記本隨你翻！著名的〈虎〉、〈倫敦〉、〈嬰兒的悲傷〉、〈枯萎的玫瑰〉等名詩手稿可放大檢視，附現代譯文、註解與語音導覽。
http://www.bl.uk/onlinegallery/ttp/ttpbooks.html

- **Blake 250**
2007年是布雷克誕生250週年紀念，英國各地紛紛舉辦向布雷克致敬的學術研討會、詩歌朗誦、音樂會與展覽活動。重新發現布雷克，有空來玩！
http://www.blake250.co.uk

- **An Island in the Moon**
線上觀賞布雷克諷刺劇《月中島》(*An Island in the Moon,* 1784)。該劇於1983年由 Joseph Viscomi 教授指導，在美國康乃爾大學公演。劇中充滿幽默的對白，其中三首詩收入《天真之歌》。
http://www.ibiblio.org/jsviscom/island

- **The Poetry Foundation**
美國現代詩基金會。創立於芝加哥，自1912年開始出版《詩刊》(*Poetry*)。厲害的是即使該社的銀行存款常少於美金100元，卻始終如期發行，不曾停刊，也一直維持良好的選詩品質，刊載過不少著名美國詩人的早期作品。2002年獲得禮來大藥廠（Eli Lilly and Company）創辦人之曾孫女 Ruth Lilly 一億美元的鉅額捐贈後，更致力於推廣詩的閱讀與教學。
http://poetryfoundation.org